THE FIFTH HORIZON

Fiora Markus

ISBN-13: 978-1-7355389-1-4

To Kevin

A Psychedelic Cowboy Legend

Prologue

Austin
(Four Years Earlier)

I had just returned to the states after spending an excruciating week and a half in London burying my stepfather and I needed a strong drink. The untimely trip had been more of an inconvenience than an emotional farewell, but I needed closure on that chapter of my life.

I also wanted the money my biological father had left my mother and I. Money that the abusive asshole who had married my mother had all but blown through after her death.

Fifty-thousand pounds.

It was hardly an amount worth making the trip for, but at least I was certain that he was absolutely *dead*.

Flicking my lit cigarette into the casket and closing the lid on that fucker had been one of the most satisfying moments of my adult life.

If there was any true justice after death, his soul was currently on its way toward spending an eternity in hell with the woman who had brought the prick into our lives in the first place.

His patient. His *special case*.

He took a beautiful, wealthy and mentally ill woman as his wife because underneath all of those fancy psychology degrees, he was even more sick than she was.

Good riddance to them both.

Nobody knew I had gone and it was better that they didn't. That was a door I would never open, least of all for the people I referred to as my friends. The truth was, I didn't have friends or enemies. I had people who would betray me eventually, and people who would betray me quickly. I preferred the latter because it was far more honest.

I had been sitting in my car grinding my teeth for twenty minutes waiting for Neil so we could hit the club early enough to get a valet spot. Parking in downtown Los Angeles on a Wednesday night was just as much of a bitch as it was any other night of the week, and the later it got the more I was beginning to lose my patience.

I pushed open the door of my Mercedes and paced to the front of the building, only to find the front door locked.

I looked at my watch; eleven o'clock.

While I had been waiting I had noticed a janitor coming and going from the side of the building, so I followed a worn foot path around to an open fire exit door.

I took the stairs up to the third floor, two at a time, turning down the dark hallway toward the video lab.

Dim light spilled out of Neil's office and I let myself in.

Neil was leaning back in his chair, stroking the dark stubble on his chin as he watched a girl through the soundproof glass wall that separated his office from the darkened video lab.

"You ready to head out?"

He didn't bother to look at me when he answered.

"Nah, she's still here."

She seemed completely unaware that Neil was watching her. *She* also seemed to be completely unaware of what time it was.

"It's already past eleven. The valet lots are going to fill up."

"Then we'll park around the block."

He gave me a dismissive wave of his hand and I felt my temperature rising.

"Piss off!" In my annoyance, I let my accent slip and had to take a moment to regroup. I had spent years trying to remove every last trace of British that still remained in me, but being in that damn country again had seeped into me like a sickness. "I'm not street parking in LA. Just tell her to go the fuck home."

He glanced up at me now, "I could, but I won't."

I had half a mind to tell the girl to get lost myself.

"Who the hell is she?"

"Her name's Brianna Rose. She's a sophomore."

"A little young for you, isn't she?"

"I'm not trying to fuck her, you moron," he sneered. "I got other plans for her."

The girl turned off her monitors, rolled her chair back, and pulled the strap of her bag over her shoulder. On her way out, she paused in the doorway of the office.

"I'm so sorry, Neil. I completely lost track of time." She tucked a strand of short, pale blonde hair behind her ear; her big eyes every bit as apologetic as her words. "Thanks for sticking around."

"Anytime, Brie," Neil replied in a voice I'd only ever heard him use with old ladies. He grinned at her with such sincerity that I doubted she knew what a shady piece of shit he was.

Her eyes then locked onto mine and she gave me an angel's smile.

I felt my mouth twitch at the corner, unable to move—*unable to fucking breathe.*

"Have a good night," she said, then disappeared from the doorway.

Neil walked toward me and shoved my shoulder with his. "A little young for you, isn't she?"

He clicked off the light and left me standing alone in the dark office.

The pounding beat of the music set the pace for my pulse. I stared at the drink in my hand—an amber backdrop to the picture of the girl whose face was still in my mind.

Neil returned to the table with a handful of assorted glasses, offering them up to everyone nearby. He was brilliant in any social setting. Always the life of the party. Straight out of Brooklyn, Neil knew how to bullshit, charm, bribe and lie to get whatever he wanted.

He was the kind of friend I kept a close eye on because I knew he would be the first to turn on me if the right opportunity arose.

"You're being a total bore tonight." Neil yelled across the table at me, pointing at my glass. "Drink up, man."

I hadn't touched a drop of my vodka and tonic, even though I had come here with the intention of drinking away the entire last week of my life. But trying to remember any thought I had ever had prior to seeing *her* seemed like a waste of mental energy.

Brianna Rose.

Neil slid his chair closer to me.

"So that girl," I raised my voice above the music. "Do you like her?"

He glanced around the room then turned back to me, "Which girl?"

"The one from the video lab."

"Who...*oh*, Brie?"

I nod, frowning at his too-familiar use of her name.

"She's cute as hell, but nah, she's not my type." He tipped back his beer. "She's fucking amazing at filmmaking, though. The piece she turned in for her freshman final?" He shook his head in awe. "She brought this homeless chick into the studio and the admin told her if she brought her in again, she'd be denied access to the studio. So she shot the entire project on a cheap handheld with shit quality in the seediest part of Los Angeles. It was a major *fuck you* to the entire department."

He lifted his eyes over my head just as a strong, familiar perfume filled my nostrils.

"What's going on boys?"

A previous hook-up named Jessica took an uninvited seat on my lap and grabbed a glass from the table.

"Neil was in the middle of telling me about a student prodigy." I looked toward Neil, making it very clear that I wanted him to finish the story, despite the unwelcome interruption.

"So anyway," Neil cleared his throat to hide his grin. "Brie got an F on the project."

"An F?" Jessica laughed. "I thought you said you were talking about a prodigy."

Her touch was as irritating to my senses as the feel of sandpaper scratching glass but I suffered in silence, wanting to shake Neil and make him finish the goddamned story.

"The final projects are always shown at the East Mal film festival and everyone—like literally *everyone*—freaked out over hers. I never like the shit that undergrads put out, but her video was fucking amazing." Neil took another long drink and glanced around the room. His eyes stopped on a thirty-something guy named Freddy, leaning over a table laughing with a couple of self-important nobodies. He wore a three-piece pinstripe suit and his hair was slicked back like a wannabe mobster. He tipped his chin at Neil who responded in return, only confirming what I already knew—that Neil was a shady motherfucker.

"So her video won something like 13 indie awards and ended up going viral."

"But she failed the class?"

"Nah," he waved it off. "She petitioned to get her grade changed, but it was the exposure she wanted more than the grade."

"So what was so great about the video?"

Neil eyed me suspiciously—I was asking too many questions.

"The homeless chick had cancer and her medical bills ended up putting her on the street. The video raised this whole social awareness issue and ended up creating so much public backlash that some hospital cleared the woman's medical debt, covered the rest of her chemo treatments and set up a medical fund for homeless people."

Jessica began to comb her fingers through my hair sensuously and I closed my eyes, trying to imagine they were *her* fingers.

Brianna Rose.

Even her name made me want to lick my lips.

"I cried, man. I fucking cried."

Neil's voice sounded choked, causing a laugh to bubble up inside of me.

"Fuck you, Austin, you heartless prick." He slammed his glass on the table top and glanced up at Jessica then back to me. He licked his bottom lip, narrowing his eyes. "You should come by the lab after I get back from Sin City next weekend. I'll introduce the two of you."

"I'll be in Barbados," I replied, never even considering the invitation. I was many things; none of which would be good for that beautiful girl.

She would have to remain an unfulfilled fantasy.

I lifted the glass to my mouth.

"Oh hey, one more thing." Neil leaned in toward my ear. "Brie's a virgin."

I choked on my drink and began to cough furiously. Alcohol dripped from my chin and nostrils, splattering all over Jessica as well as my pants. I shoved her from my lap, leaving her glaring and cursing up at me from the floor.

"Fu-huck!" I coughed, beating my fist against my chest, trying to ease the burning sensation that seared the top of my windpipe and my nose.

I gasped in a long breath, giving zero fucks that everyone around us was watching me die a slow and humiliating death by permanent erection.

"Are you fucking serious?" I finally managed to choke out in a broken voice.

Neil could barely catch his breath for laughing so hard. "So fucking predictable."

"You're a piece of shit, Malone!" I shoved away from the table and stood up, grabbing my coat from the back of my chair. "Get your own ride home!"

Austin

(Present)

Outside of that one captured moment between us, Brianna never even knew I existed.

She had become a beautiful temptation.

On occasion, I found myself following her to the coffee shop where she worked, but had never entered the shop until this morning.

I craved seeing her, and despite knowing that our story could never end well, I pulled open the door, ordered a coffee and hid myself at a table by the window, pretending to read a newspaper.

I allowed myself to watch her as she moved from table to table, chatting with her co-worker.

"I registered for my last two classes so all I need is a studio internship and if everything works out, I'll have my degree by the end of the semester."

Brianna was cleaning the table behind me when she accidentally bumped her shoulder against mine and placed her hand on my arm apologetically, "I'm so sorry."

Her smell hypnotized me with an enchanting mix of

hazelnut coffee with a hint of patchouli.

I was torn from the shadows of her life and unexpectedly pulled into the light. I lifted my hand and cleared my throat uncomfortably.

"It's alright." I said, lifting my eyes to her as my fingers trembled unnoticeably around my coffee cup. "Did you say you're a film student?"

She nodded, "Yes; a grad student at East Mal."

It was clear she didn't remember me from the night in the lab all those years earlier, but there was no reason she should.

"Murray Studios is looking for a production intern. We haven't advertised for the position yet, but if you're interested I'll have our production manager get in touch with you."

We hadn't advertised for it because no such position existed.

Murray Studios wasn't one of the production powerhouses that Hollywood was known for, but I had helped carve out a name for it by producing a few successful television shows since partnering with Jack Murray. If she was a film student, she had heard of my studio.

She clutched the washcloth in her hand, bringing it to her chest, "Oh my gosh, are you serious?"

I smiled at her, "Of course."

Her eyes dilated as she studied my face.

She was so dangerously close. I could reach out and stroke her cheek with my fingers—touch the beautiful face I had dreamed about so many nights and had resisted for so many years.

This was a terrible mistake.

One touch of her own hand had already brought me too close to temptation. The light was on my face. I was exposed and this time she would not as easily forget. The only way to go with her now was forward. A chill of both anticipation and fear passed though me as I considered what that meant for the two of us.

"Will you be working here tomorrow?" I asked, already knowing the answer.

"Yes, from 5 until 1." She held out her hand to me. "My name's Brianna."

"Brianna," I repeated, tasting her name as I took her hand, feeling my heart throbbing heavily at the top of my throat. "I'm Austin."

"It's so nice to meet you, Austin." When she smiled, her dimple destroyed the last of my resolve to keep away from her.

"I have to leave, but I'll have someone bring the paperwork by for you tomorrow morning."

"I don't want you to have to go to any trouble. I'd be happy to come by the studio."

"It's no trouble at all."

"Thank you so much," she smiled again. "I really appreciate your kindness."

Mercifully, another customer took her attention away from me, leaving me to close my eyes and breathe deeply, still feeling the ghost of her hand in mine.

What had I done?

Brianna

"Brie, I think we're out of cups!"

I smiled at the customer standing in front of me, "Your total is five dollars and fifty-three cents."

The older gentleman handed me his credit card, glancing over my shoulder at my pacing co-worker as I slid his card into the reader.

He leaned forward and whispered, "You might want to cut back on her caffeine."

I handed him back his card.

"We go through this every day," I replied quietly. "Yesterday it was creamers."

"Brianna!" Gabby hissed my name, now in a full panic.

"Have a nice day!" I said, sending the man on his way with his coffee and a smile, leaving the shop empty except for the two of us.

I turned to Gabby and my smile dropped. "Gabby, we are not out of cups. Please stop freaking out in front of the customers."

She sat on an empty milk crate with her face between her hands as she tried to keep herself from hyperventilating. She had a tendency to overreact about things, but ever since she had switched to the morning shift, her anxiety over the simplest things had become nearly unbearable.

I brushed past her into the storage closet and came back with a case of cups, dropping them at her feet. "See? We're fine."

She looked up at me, wide-eyed, "Where did you get those?"

I pulled my apron over my head. "They magically appeared on the shelf marked *coffee cups*."

Chase plowed through the front door wearing tiny blue mirrored sunglasses, his matching blue hair a mess of spikes. He draped his arm around my shoulder and leaned his head against mine, both of us now staring down at Gabby.

"Baby," Chase purred into my ear, smelling of vanilla. "Is Gabby freaking out again?"

"You came to work hungover?" I turned and gently pushed him away while he flashed a lazy grin at me. Chase was my first friend in California. I had met him when I had started working at the coffee shop during my freshman year at East Mal and over the years we had helped each other through our fair share of early morning hangovers.

"Seriously," Gabby huffed, interrupting what would have likely turned into a lecture. "I can't handle first shift anymore. Lora needs to switch back."

"She needs the late shift right now," I said, rubbing her back sympathetically. "She has to take care of her kids in the morning until she finds a new sitter."

"Ugh!" Gabby groaned. "Why do people have kids?"

Chase laughed inappropriately loud, making me elbow him.

"It's just a temporary switch," I promised. "In two weeks you'll be starting the afternoon shift with Chase."

Chase bit at the metal stud in his lower lip and wiggled a pierced eyebrow at her.

I gave him a disapproving lift of my eyebrow and he grinned at me. "Don't be jealous, baby. Just say the word and you know I'd be yours."

I placed a comforting hand on Gabby's shoulder. "Go home and get some sleep, Gabs."

I grabbed a water bottle and muffin and began walking toward the door.

Chase trailed after me. "Off to kick it with the rich and famous?"

I snorted, "If you mean cater to, clean up after and do nothing even remotely close to what I'm getting my degree in, then yes."

"And all for free."

"Right," I laughed, pushing the front door open. "Make sure Gabby's okay."

"Comforting women is what I do best."

"Don't hit on her."

"It's only ever been you, Brie," He kissed my cheek.

"Dream big, Chase," I said, placing a hand on his cheek before walking out.

I could still hear his laughter even as the door closed behind me.

The newspaper that our neighborhood homeless man was using for a blanket lifted slightly in the breeze, showing me that he was asleep. I placed the wrapped muffin and water bottle on his bench before I continued on my way toward the Metro.

I have looked at homelessness so differently since getting to know Mika.

Everyone has a story, but the homeless tend to have ones that people don't want to hear. Sometimes they're too painful to listen to and sometimes they make you feel guilty for taking your own blessings for granted. It's always heartbreaking to see another human being in need, so we often convince ourselves it's somehow *their* fault. That it's addiction or mental illness or laziness. But sometimes it's just bad luck, a bad series of life events—a deep hole of debt with no ladder…

I know I don't have the power to change the world, but every time I leave someone a bottle of water and a muffin, or meet their eyes with a genuine smile that conveys that everyone is worthy of a little kindness; I think of *The Star Thrower* and remember *to that one person* I can make a difference.

Earlier in the semester Austin had been true to his word and had sent me an offer for the production internship without even asking about my experience or qualifications.

Trying to make industry connections without having a foot on the first rung would have been an insurmountable task, but by some strange twist of fate Austin had appeared in my life at the right time and the internship just fell in place.

Internships in this field were extremely competitive, and even though most of what I did in the position had very little to do with my career goals, I enjoyed the entire experience.

I didn't plan on staying in Hollywood after I graduated, though I had no idea what I would be doing next. I had watched so many people struggling to make it in a place where filmmakers were a dime a dozen, but the ones who had found success had left L.A. as soon as they graduated.

I was two weeks away from finishing my internship and completing all of my graduate requirements. After spending the last six years in school, I was more than ready to be moving on from that chapter of my life and begin doing something that mattered.

What Murray Studios did was as far from what I wanted to be doing as possible. In fact, they were about to start filming on a show that went against everything I believed in: love, marriage, and women making fools of themselves for a man's attention.

Even the thought of the show made me want to spit the coffee that was still warming my mouth at the men behind the project. But who was I? Just a bright-eyed, inexperienced film student who still valued quality of content over the almighty dollar—a virtual *sin* in Hollywood.

Though I had been given the chance to speak my mind about the new show—a courtesy that most interns did not get —I hadn't been eloquent enough to sway anyone's opinion.

I had been completely blindsided by the question, to be honest.

Austin, the man from the coffee shop, turned out to be the CEO of Murray Studios as well as the executive producer. He was the big boss—second only to some silent, hands-off investor who lived in Barbados.

Austin was young, rich, untouchably gorgeous, and hadn't spoken a single word to me since that day in the coffee shop.

At first I thought I had somehow offended him, but the longer I worked there the more I realized he didn't talk to most people unless he absolutely had to. When he did speak, he was generally soft-spoken but he still managed to reek of power and confidence. His eyes often spoke volumes where his mouth remained silent.

"Brianna," Austin had stopped me on the day the idea for the new show had been revealed to the staff. He quirked a smile at me. "What are your thoughts about the new show?"

"Oh...well," I hesitated, trying to choose my words carefully. "I'm not really an expert in viewer preferences."

"I want to know *your* thoughts," he clarified.

Under his intoxicating gaze, I could feel how easy it would be to tell him whatever he wanted. To just say, "It's brilliant! You're a conceptual genius."

But that was total bullshit.

The idea for the show genuinely sucked, and I had no vested interest in kissing his sexy, rich ass. Nor did I have any hope of getting a huge bonus if the project was, by some miracle, not a total failure. Hell, I wasn't even getting paid to do what I already did.

Considering all of this in under three seconds, I decided to go for being completely honest and let my mouth take the wheel.

"Well, as you had said, the show is going to be called *Mistery Marriage*. To be honest, just trying to get past the intentional misspelling of 'mystery' is a bit of an uphill battle for me. It's alphabet abuse. Y already gets a raw deal in the whole vowels versus consonants debate. *Sometimes* Y. But only sometimes. Like in the word mystery. Messing with the spelling won't make up for the fact that the entire concept of the show is a sexist pile of crap."

At this point, he was smirking so hard his face began turning pink from holding it back. The yes-man at his side stared at me like I had completely lost my mind.

I had just insulted the CEO to his face and had used the actual phrase *sexist pile of crap* to describe his brainchild.

He had made it very clear that he wanted *my* opinion and I owed him the courtesy of the truth, despite how mortified I felt after having done so.

"I agree with you. Unfortunately several other studios have similar ideas in the works so we have to be the ones to do it first." The casual grin appearing on his face made my heart stop. "But thank you for speaking so openly—your honesty is very much appreciated."

Austin made no further mention of my candid comment. However, since then, instead of looking away when our eyes met—he held them, letting a knowing smile tug at his lips.

Whatever I had broken in him, I was glad of it.

* * *

I arrived at the studio straight from my shift at the coffee shop that Friday afternoon.

I changed out of my barista clothes and into my intern uniform: skinny jeans and a black fitted v-neck tee with the words FREE HELP printed on the back.

I knew it was intended to be funny, and I wasn't ungrateful for the opportunity, but I so desperately could have used a paid internship.

I was extremely fortunate that my tuition had been covered and I wouldn't be drowning in student loan debt for the rest of my life. But just trying to cover the cost of rent for a small studio apartment meant that on most months I could barely cover my bills.

On days when tips were given more generously at the coffee shop, I could afford to treat myself to little luxuries, like cheap bath towels to replace the ones that were threadbare.

I tucked my purse and clothes into my staff locker and stuffed the key into my pocket, stopping at a mirror to comb through my chin length pixie cut with my fingers.

"Brie!"

I turned to find the studio's production manager in the doorway.

Joelle was my immediate supervisor, and it took a lot to fluster her. Yet there she stood with her face flushed and her calm composure hanging on by a thread.

"Those girls!" She hissed at me wide-eyed. "I just can't!"

"What girls?" I giggled without meaning to.

"The contestants."

Ah. The women who would be competing to marry the celebrity bachelor on the new show that is *not* being brought to viewers by the letter Y.

"They're in wardrobe. They were so obnoxious that Wanda nearly threw them out of makeup." She shoved a clipboard into my hands. "Can you take these papers to Austin or Heath for me? I have to get back in there to make sure Fabiano doesn't go homicidal."

"Of course," I took the papers and turned toward the set as she slipped into another room.

"Your name is going to be on the lips of every person in America!"

The honey-coated words of Full-of-Shit Phil, the studio's a-hole APOC, floated down the hall, making me cringe. By the way he spoke, I assumed he was talking to the celebrity bachelor they had chosen for the first season of the show. *The mystery mister,* I giggled to myself rolling my eyes at nobody.

The man's identity was a highly guarded secret, so to avoid media leaks, very few people had been privy to this information beforehand. Even most of the staff had been kept in the dark until the last possible moment.

I paused and stepped aside to let Phil and the mystery man pass as they moved down the hall toward his dressing room.

The two men passed me by without even so much as a glance my way, like I was completely invisible. Not even a blip on their female radar. Not that I wanted to be.

Kevin "Trax" Thomas, *a.k.a. the god of grunge,* was the frontman for the band Chevron Dreams. I didn't know much else about him except that he had a reputation for never dating the same woman twice.

The fact that a perpetually single man like him was participating in a show where the very premise was to end up marrying one of the women contestants, I had to wonder just how desperate for publicity he was.

As I continued toward the set, I began counting backwards the number of days I still had left in my internship and would no longer have to witness first-hand the train wreck that this show was going to be.

Trax

When Freddy's meeting about *a great fucking opportunity* began with him handing me a glass of Gentleman Jack, I should have known right then and there that he was going to screw me so hard my ass would feel it for months.

After all the resistance I put up against doing interviews and other media bullshit, it should have been a no-brainer to turn this *great fucking opportunity* down.

He knows damn well how uncomfortable I get out of my element.

Give me a guitar and a mic, and twenty thousand fans merge into an extension of myself that I can handle without even blinking an eye. They're there for us, and all the positive energy gets me through the few hours we're up on stage performing each night.

But put me in a smaller setting and I just shrink right into myself.

Randy Eller, our band's lead guitarist, has always been the voice of Chevron Dreams. Not only because he's got an easy, outgoing personality, but because I decline every single interview request and someone needs to promote the band.

I'm the frontman—the face of the band—so it's almost

always *me* they want. But unless I'm asked a direct question or feel compelled to speak, I prefer to just sit back and keep my mouth shut.

Those few times I had given an interview, my words had come out low and quiet, so the media mislabelled my introversion as disinterested broodiness when in fact I'm just too fucking terrified to speak.

My bandmates call me the loudmouth mute; loud and outgoing with people I know and dead silent with those I don't.

This makes promoting the band a job that sucks fifty asses, and right now I'd willingly sit through just about any interview if I could find a way out of doing this show.

Hell, I really just want to get out of this room.

My nerves are kicking my ass, and my tell is that I'm bouncing my knee and pounding a beat out on my legs with my thumbs.

The dude with the bad hair plugs who I've been stuck on this particular level of hell with for the past hour hasn't stopped kissing my ass for one minute.

I'm damn close to faking having to take a piss just to get him to shut the hell up, but he'd probably follow me to the bathroom and praise me for what a great fucking job I did pissing.

I scratch my scruff-stubbled cheek for the fifth time.

It's probably not the best time to be growing out my beard again, but screw it. I'm lazy enough to make the look work in my favor.

My irritation is co-writing a melody that keeps biting at the inside of my mind on repeat, so I hum it out, keeping the words trapped behind my closed lips.

"I know what you're concerned about," Stan, or Bob, or what the hell is his name?...*Phil*...interrupts my song.

I glance over at him, lifting a skeptical eyebrow.

"You don't have to marry any of them..."

Yeah, no shit. I've heard this already.

And in the words of Freddy, 'since I'm already committed to this show, I could at least fake an interest over the next eight weeks for the amount of money they're paying me'.

Problem with that is, I don't know how to fake something like that.

I've never been in love, and I don't see myself falling in love anytime soon.

I'm not opposed to the idea, I just don't live in an environment that's very conducive to love happening.

Groupies aren't keepers, the women on our crew don't like dick, reporters flirt with every damn celebrity they meet and everyone else comes and goes too quickly to get to know on a deeper level.

Being single has worked for me so far and I imagine it will keep working for me as long as the band is still touring. Unfortunately, never having been known to have a serious girlfriend has earned me the reputation of being a man-whore, which is complete bullshit.

Did I sleep with random chicks? Yeah—right along with a whole lot of other indulgent shit that people do when they're shot to instant fame in their early twenties.

Do I still do all that shit? *Fuck no.*

Unfortunately, the public's perception is stuck on the old me and the misconception that I am somehow committed to my bachelor status made me the perfect mark for the producers of this show. Freddy went and signed my ass up without even asking me.

The goal, he says, is to get the band back in the headlines right before our tour kicks off at the end of the summer.

So my job is to show up, play nice, and somehow make fans out of people who don't already listen to our music.

I have no idea how that reasoning works out, but I highly

doubt that this bullshit is going to directly translate into higher album, merch and ticket sales.

"…unless you make a real love connection."

Took the guy long enough to finally spit that out.

I chuckled out loud.

If I had to guess by the smirk he was holding back, even he didn't believe that shit.

Love connection.

You gotta be fucking kidding me.

I looked down at a text that had just come through.

RANDY: Clearwater put up 100k for Marietta if you actually marry one of those chicks

I ran my hand over my face, feeling the weight of his words.

Randy's sister was diagnosed with breast cancer at The Marietta Center two years ago, and my mom… I shake my head, pushing away the thought. Rich Clearwater, the music producer at our label, R3 Records, is one of the few people who knows it's my ass on the line to be married. He's been taking every chance he gets to taunt me about getting hitched.

It ain't gonna happen.

RANDY: He's challenging everyone at R3 to match it

TRAX: Of course he is

RANDY: Pretty sure we're at half a mil now - no pressure

TRAX: (middle finger emoji)

I blew out a long breath and shoved my phone back into my pocket.

This was supposed to be a public relations gig, not a fucking fundraiser.

I scratched at my chest nervously, glancing over at the door like I was being held against my will, just waiting for the chance to make a break.

I wondered what the odds were that any of these women would be tolerable enough to marry.

I snorted out a laugh, making the weasel look in my direction.

Brianna

On any given day, Austin's messy brown undercut alone could do me in. But today his eyes were the killers—so deep in concentration as Tilly spoke to him at a near-frantic pace.

I bit my bottom lip as I watched him standing with his arms crossed over his chest, the top button of his shirt undone and his tie hanging loosely around his neck—he was truly breathtaking.

With only two hours left before filming began, I was forced to ruin the beautiful sight.

"Excuse me," I said when Tilly had taken a pause in speaking.

Austin glanced at me over Tilly's shoulder, his stiff posture quickly relaxing.

"Brianna?" Austin gave me an easy smile. "Something I can do for you?"

I held out the clip board. "Joelle asked me to bring these papers to you. She's stuck in wardrobe."

"Perfect. Thank you," He took the clipboard from me and I turned to walk away.

"We have nobody else. We're going to have to postpone..." I heard Tilly say, but Austin cut her off. "Wait, wait, wait...

Brianna…"

Hearing my name, I turned around.

Austin stared at me for a long moment, "What about Brianna?"

Tilly's expression shifted as she studied me, tapping her chin with a pen. "She's nothing at all like the other two."

Other two?

The hint of a smile lingered just beneath the surface of Austin's expression.

"She is pretty," Tilly observed. "But his bio sheet made it abundantly clear that he prefers large…" She held her hands far in front of her chest to illustrate her meaning. "No offense, Brie."

"Uh, none taken?" I said with uncertainty.

Austin's eyes remained on mine and he slowly slid his tongue over his lower lip in a way that nearly ruined me for all other men.

"We don't want him to choose her," he finally said. "We just need her to fill the seat."

I felt my pulse quickening as I began to realize what they were considering asking me to do.

"If he does pick her the viewers are going to flip!" Tilly laughed, creating a headline in the air with her hand. "Girl next door tames bad boy rocker."

"Oh no," I began shaking my head, backing away from them. "No, no, no…I can't."

Austin moved toward me as I retreated, matching me step for step with his charming smile.

"I can't get married, Austin," I insisted.

He slid his arm around my shoulder.

"All we're asking you to do is be a warm body in chair number three. The third girl we had cast bailed on us this morning and there's no time to find someone else. You're the only one in the studio who even comes close to who we would need."

"So I won't actually have to marry him?"

"Let's just say there's an extremely low chance you would have to marry him."

I cringed.

Austin added. "The studio was provided with a list of very specific qualities he prefers in a woman so that we could cast people appropriate to his tastes. It's highly unlikely that he'll pick you based on some of the qualities listed on that sheet; he prefers long blonde hair for example…"

"…and big ta-tas," Tilly chimes in.

"… and he likely would not be drawn to you because you have a great deal of self respect."

Well, there's that.

"But what if he does pick me?"

"He'd have to choose you in at least two of the three competition rounds for that to even become a possibility."

"Aaand…what if he does pick me?" I repeated my question and he grinned at me.

"Then yes, according to the contract, you'd be obligated to marry him."

I shook my head, "Nope."

"But again…" he quickly assured me, placing his hands on my arms. "That's an extremely unlikely scenario."

"I can't marry him," I nearly whispered. "Please, Austin."

"Brianna," he melted me with his gaze and took my hand gently between his. "If I thought there was any real risk that you'd have to marry this man, I wouldn't even consider asking. If you do this for us, the studio will compensate you as they would an acting professional."

"This isn't acting—*it's marriage!*" I replied. "An actual, legitimate marriage contract!"

"I know," he said, closing his eyes as if he sympathized with me. "Brianna, this is the pilot episode. If we have to halt production and the pilot fails to air after all the hype, we'll have broken contract with our sponsors. We'll still have to meet the financial obligations of our contracts and all the celebrities we've already hired through the first season, the advertising venues, the air time... Not to mention that we'd be responsible for the lost jobs and income of the entire team involved in production. It would be a lot more cost effective for us to pay you to fill in than to pay our lawyers and accountants to clean up after a cancelled show."

I frowned.

"I highly doubt that the man we've hired to be the bachelor for this season is planning to leave the show with a wife. It's all about getting publicity. Please, Brianna," he lowered his chin, looking up at me through long eyelashes. "Will you do this for me?"

He had sealed the deal with my loins the moment he took my hand in his—I just needed my brain to catch up.

I sighed.

"Okay." I said, trying to convince myself the right thing to do didn't always feel that way. And they were right—there was no way Trax Thomas would ever want to marry me. He had to be more than a decade older than me. I had absolutely nothing a guy like him wanted, and of that...I was thankful.

"Snow White ain't nowhere near as pale as you look right now, honey."

I groaned, dropping my face into my hands, "Why am I doing this, Wanda?"

"Because that man can sweet talk the pants off a nun." She replied, flinging her makeup brush around. "Now put those hands down and let me do my job."

"I'm not used to wearing makeup." I complained. "It makes me feel so fake."

"Hmm, you want fake? Wait until you see those two

women they got you going up against. They pretty and all, but they both look like they fresh outta Dee Snyder beauty school."

I snorted out a laugh as I began to flip through pages of the thick contract on my lap.

"I have no idea what I'm even looking at here. I don't want to end up signing away the rights to my first born or anything."

"I'm sure that man would love for you to have his babies," she mumbled under her breath.

I peered up at her and she snatched the contract from my hand. She flipped through a few pages until she found what she was looking for then folded it over and handed it back to me, tapping the paper with a comb. "Right there..." she said, beginning work on my hair. "...that's the only page that specifically pertains to you. All the rest is lawyer-speak, and if Chevron's fancy-ass lawyers signed off on it, there's no reason to believe anything shady's going on. Besides, Austin ain't about to screw you over or it might mess up his chances at screwing you for reals."

"What do you mean?"

She quirked an eyebrow at me, "Tell me you ain't as dumb as you look right now."

My mouth opened slightly then closed again in confusion.

She rolled her eyes, "*Please*. That man's got it bad for you."

"What? Who does?"

"The big man. *Duh*. And if things don't work out with Eddie Van Halen out there...Austin's hot, is all I'm sayin'."

I looked back down at the contract and suddenly gasped, jumping from the chair and clutching my robe at the chest.

"Holy shit!" I exclaimed, staring wide-eyed at the paper.

Wanda yelled out, "What is it? What's wrong?"

My mouth hung open in shock, "Four hundred thousand dollars an episode?"

Her eyes narrowed in amusement as she grinned back at me, "Welcome to Hollywood, Miss Brie. Check your morals at the door and get ready for the ride of your life because that man is hot for your ass." She tapped the chair, "Now sit down. We got work to do."

I tugged at the gray plaid skater skirt Fabiano had chosen for me to wear.

I wasn't used to short skirts—or any skirts, really.

It was awkward enough that he had to hand me a razor and tell me to shave my wooly mammoth legs while we were in there. Razors aren't cheap and I've had to use them sparingly. It's much less expensive to wear jeans and pretend that I wasn't actively growing my own knee-socks.

I drew my line with the heels, though. No amount of money was worth killing myself on heels, so instead, he let me wear a pair of shin-high lime green combat boots. With my pixie-bob naturally red hair dyed pure white, I felt like Tinkerbell's punk rock sister.

I could feel Austin's gaze on me as I crossed the set toward my chair.

After Wanda's comment, I was suddenly more aware of him and it made my skin flush.

If she was right, and my bosses bosses bosses boss was attracted to me, then I had a very real problem.

I just wanted to leave this company with some studio experience, a reference, and my internship credits—not a whirlwind love affair with the young, super hot CEO.

It made me uncomfortable to think he was paying any more attention to me than anyone else.

I wasn't a big fan of attention.

Ironic, since I was about to receive all sorts of attention, having to pretend to be vying for a chance to marry Hottie McRockstar.

The idea of competing for marriage didn't sit well with me. Nor did the fraction of a chance that I might be contractually obligated to marry the guy.

But four-hundred thousand dollars an episode was a hell of a lot of new bath towels, and I really needed the financial breathing room if I was going to pick up after graduation and move to who knows where and live for who knows how long without a paying job.

I noticed my competition eyeing me. Both of them were deeply tanned, busty bleach-blondes with skinny waists and lip injections.

I laughed inwardly.

Hand-picked to suit his taste, indeed.

Heaven only knows what they were thinking about me.

"Episode one will be a blind competition round," Austin began to explain as he paced in front of the set.

A four-sided, textured plexiglass partition separated Trax from the area where the women sat.

His blurred figure could be seen inside, leaning back with crossed arms, looking almost annoyed at having to be there. To my relief, he didn't look like a man eager to take home a wife.

"In today's episode," Austin continued, "Our celebrity bachelor's identity will remain completely anonymous to you as well as the viewers until his reveal at the end of tonight's episode. After asking the three of you a series of pre-determined questions, he will then choose the woman he feels most attracted to, sight-unseen."

Austin's eyes lingered for a moment on mine before he continued.

"A date with the winner of this round will follow as next week's episode, and the following week we will all return to film the second competition round, which will be held in the same manner as a beauty pageant. Our bachelor will choose one of you based on visual appearance and sense of style."

I let a quick laugh escape involuntarily and Austin paused as he glanced over at me.

"You will be wearing formal wear, club wear, and lounge wear. You will not be permitted to compete in anything too revealing."

One of the other two girls sighed and looked down at her painted nails in boredom.

"Round two will be followed by a date with the winner of that round, and then that will be followed by the third competition round which will showcase your domestic talents. You will each treat our bachelor to a home cooked meal, a mixed drink, and a massage."

The other girl quickly raised her hand and Austin pointed to her, "And the answer to *that* question is *no*."

Her shoulders slumped and a frown overtook her face.

"This show will be aired with a rating of ages 13 and up, so let's try to keep that in mind, shall we?"

He paced toward my end of the set again, his eyes holding mine the entire way.

How had I never noticed before?

"The winner of each round will accompany our bachelor on a date of his arranging and the entire date will be filmed."

The first girl raised her hand. "If we all get to date him, does that mean we all get to marry him?"

Austin placed his hand on the arm of my chair in frustration.

"We are not in Utah, Tiffinni."

"Yeah, I don't know what that means," she replied.

I could see the shadow of Trax slowly shaking his head and I inwardly chuckled. Maybe he wasn't such a bad guy if he was able to find the humor in all of this.

"It means," Austin sighed loudly, "that only the winner of

each round goes on a date with him, and if he chooses the same woman in two rounds, he can either choose to marry her or remain a bachelor. If he chooses her in all three rounds, then that woman automatically becomes his bride."

"So you mean he can just choose not to marry us?" the same girl protests.

Austin pushed away from my chair, running a hand through his hair in frustration.

"The rules are very clearly spelled out in the contracts each of you signed. You are not guaranteed to leave this show with a husband. If you would like to do so, you should try your best to win in the competition rounds."

The show's director, Heath, came rushing into the studio and Austin walked off the set. The two men spent a moment speaking quietly with one another, then time began counting down.

"Is everybody ready? Quiet on the set!" Someone said, causing my two competitors to begin primping. "5…4…3," He pointed down 2 then the show's host jumped in front of the camera like the caffeine and crack he had for dinner had just kicked in.

My mind began to wander as he went over the same concept of the show for the viewers, but in a much more animated tone than Austin had.

I tried to forget that the entire country would be on the other end of that camera lens, watching me pimp myself out for a prize I didn't even want. I was the underdog.

That would become clear to everyone watching—especially when they found out that Trax Thomas was the man behind the plexiglass.

I glanced over at the other two contestants.

Barely a full brain between the two of them.

They were exactly the kind of women a rock star would want on his arm.

All I had to do was sit back and be the most snarky, uptight, annoyingly brainy person I could be for the next seven weeks. Easy peasy lemon squeezy.

I cracked my knuckles pushing outwardly on my laced fingers, ready to channel my inner smart-ass.

It's showtime.

Trax

"Tiffinni," I cringe at the spelling of her name.

Lifting the first card and reading it, like I had been instructed to.

"If you could change one thing about the world, what would you change?"

I roll my eyes, my attitude getting shittier by the minute as I consider to myself that any chick with a name spelled *t-i-f-f-i-n-n-i* probably couldn't change a roll of toilet paper, let alone the world.

One of the women, presumably Tiffinni, answers my question.

"Well," she giggles like a toddler and I almost groan at the predictability of the woman. Why the hell did I let Freddy fill out the questionnaire about what kind of women I go for? I had been so pissed about him signing me up for this shit that I couldn't be bothered to take it seriously, and now I was going to suffer. "I would take away the clothing restrictions on public beaches."

I was ten seconds from standing up and walking out, but I let her words sink in and couldn't seem to let it go.

Was this chick just fucking with me? Or did she actually mean this shit?

I cleared my throat, trying to find the voice that wanted to hide.

These were my own unscripted thoughts now, and that's where my words usually got stuck.

"Can you clarify what you mean by clothing restrictions?"

I heard her hesitate.

"Um, you know how like beaches make you wear shoes and stuff? Like in the shops and restaurants and stuff? Those restrictions. I'd totally take them away. No more shoes at the beach—*woo!*"

She fucking *woo'ed.*

I placed my hand to my forehead and squeezed.

"Have you ever walked on hot sand, Tiff?" I mumbled. I've burned the bottoms of my feet raw walking on sand dunes while I was drunk way more than I care to admit.

"Um… no?"

"Got it," I replied. I guess that's a lesson *T-i-f-f-i-n-n-i* will have to learn for herself.

I heard a voice in my ear piece, "Move on to Brandi."

"Had to ask…okay," I looked at the name card and shook my head.

Brandi. *Really?*

The intellectual failings of this generation can be blamed on parents who spell their kids names wrong intentionally. It's not unique and memorable; it's confusing as shit.

If your daughter's name ends with an *i* and you aren't French? You're a bad. fucking. parent.

"Brandi, how about you? If you could change one thing about the world, what would you change?"

Aside from the spelling of your name.

"I would get rid of stop signs." *Fuck.* "And red lights." I hang my head. "They only slow people down, you know? They're always holding everyone up. I mean, I try to get to the gym and I legit have to stop my car like fifty times. It's so ridiculous. But take away all the stop signs and red lights and —*boom!*—it's a straight shot to anywhere."

"Yeah, *boom* is right," I chuckle, now leaning forward on my elbows and twirling my thumb ring. "So you're opposed to stop signs. Are you also opposed to railroad crossing signals?"

"Definitely."

"I see."

Did they really expect me to marry one of these chicks?

Back in the dressing room I had almost been tempted to consider it after I had gotten the text about Marietta. But I have my limits and these women have stumbled way past them.

Only seven more weeks. I can get through this. I hope.

I look down at the third chick's name.

Brianna.

Not Breyahna or Brihannah—well, that's hopeful.

"Brianna," I say, expecting the worst. I arced and shuffled the index cards in my hand like a deck of playing cards, trying to use up some of my nervous energy. "Same question as Tiffinni and Brandi."

The third chick replied, "I'd make it a priority that everyone learned how to read and speak in multiple languages."

As I began to arc them again her words hit me and the index cards shot from my hands into the air, scattering all over the floor.

The fuck did she just say?

"Can you elaborate?"

I slid forward on my seat and began collecting the cards from the floor, trying to put them back in order. I knew I was pushing my luck by asking her to elaborate, but what the hell.

"Culturally literate people with diverse communication

skills are far more likely to change the world than one person on a TV show and are far less likely to tamper with restrictions that have been put in place for health and public safety."

I snorted.

"Right on."

Her dig at the other chicks was subtle enough that they didn't pick up on it. Seems bachelorette number three was smart, rude, *and feisty*.

If she was also cute, well, shit!

I whipped out the next card in the stack

"Tiffinni," I said, with a little more enthusiasm. "What's your favorite number?"

"Sixty-nine," she giggled again like a seven year old.

Of course it is.

"How about you, Brandi?"

"Sixty-nine." She answered quickly, like she was enthusiastically guessing the answer, hoping she was right.

"Brianna?" I asked, hoping she wouldn't disappoint me.

"One."

"Okay," I grinned, hopefully. "So I get the meaning of Tiffinni and Brandi's answers—care to explain yours?"

"One is the most emotionally conflicting number there is. People strive to be number one while at the same time pray that they don't end up single."

How the hell did this woman make the final cut if they were using Freddy's list?

That small extroverted part of me which usually hides in the shadows until I'm stone drunk was shoving my introverted ass to the side, wanting to ask this woman more questions just to see what she would say next. Every answer seemed calculated, like she was intentionally trying to be off-putting, yet her words came out almost lyrical.

She had me on the line before I even knew what hit me—I

was fucking intrigued.

"We're on commercial," the voice in my ear piece says.

"So how hot is this Brianna chick?" I quietly ask the voice.

He laughed, "Sorry man—can't help you in this round."

I glance down at the third question but I know I've already chosen Brianna before I even ask it.

Even though a part of me is looking forward to meeting the woman face to face, I'm also not stupid. Just because her answers suggest that she's rockin' a little more brains than the other two doesn't mean she's gonna be nice to look at. It's almost a guarantee that she'll be average, at best. That's the way these shows work; they set you up to choose between brains and beauty just to prove that you're a shallow fuck when you choose beauty the next time around.

Classic Hollywood bullshit.

I hear the show's host just before the voice in my ear piece says, "Go ahead and ask the next question."

"Tiffinni, this question is for you. Where's your ideal vacation spot?"

"Oh, it's totally Paris. It's such an awesome college, you know?"

I tilt my head—*did she understand the question?*

"Have you ever been to Paris, Tiffinni?"

"I have! Go Irish! *Woo!*"

I cringe as the puzzle comes together.

Notre Dame…

I consider the possibility of this woman bringing children into the world and send up a silent prayer that the man she procreates with will be wealthy enough to hire someone to guide their children into the world of basic intelligence.

After a long pause, I shake my head to clear my thoughts.

"Brandi, how about you?"

"My ideal vacation spot is the beach."

"Just out of curiosity," I heard Brianna jump in,

unprompted. "Are we talking about the actual beach? Or the zen-like shoe-free boardwalk?"

I cackle out a loud laugh.

"Brie's on fire and Tiffinni just got burned," I overhear them whispering and laughing behind the set in my ear piece.

"What would you even know?" Tiffinni bit out in response to Brianna's dig. "People who look like you shouldn't go anywhere near the beach."

"That's right," Brandi adds in solidarity.

People who look like you?

Well, shit.

That doesn't fare well for Brianna being hot, but fuck it—she's funny enough. Maybe we could just go someplace dark for our date…hit the movies or maybe a planetarium.

Double shit.

Ugly would be hard to get over.

Hell, maybe if I'm lucky she's just small chested or a book nerd.

I was always hot for chicks like that. I'm more of an ass guy anyway, and needless to say book nerds are in short supply backstage at concerts.

"Brianna—" I say, pushing the distraction from my mind. "Your ideal vacation spot?"

"Home," she replies, sealing the fucking deal for me. "I've lived in SoCal for five years, so I'm a little vacationed out."

Introvert me high-fives extrovert me.

"So going out on tour with me…?" I just threw that out there and I have no idea why.

"…would be my idea of hell." She answered.

Wide-eyed, I blew out a long breath from my inflated cheeks.

"Last question."

The need to see what this chick looked like had me feeling

all kinds of fucked up and I had no idea why. I knew it was probably going to be like a kick to the nuts when I finally saw her, but not knowing for sure was a real bitch. I wanted to check my delusions at the door, because I was only twenty minutes in and already feeling invested in her.

"Tiffinni…why should I choose you to be my wife?"

As usual, she didn't hesitate to answer.

"Because I would fulfill your every fantasy."

Fifteen years ago that might have been the correct answer, but at my age and after having been in the spotlight for so long, I'm just too damn jaded by shit like that.

My fantasy right now is to be a normal fucking guy. And normal fucking guys don't get sex shoved in their face 24/7. Normal guys don't end up on television shows selling their self respect for a little fucking publicity. They end up with small-chested book nerds and have families and dogs and they live happily ever after.

Rock stars—we have to fight for every moment of the life that normal people get to experience every day.

So sorry, Tiffinni, but I'm pretty sure you wouldn't be able to fulfill shit for me.

"Brandi, how about you?"

"I would just die if I could be a celebrity's wife. My friends would be so jealous and I'd get to sit around the pool in the sun all day and never have to work or anything. It would be so awesome."

"*So awesome,*" Tiffinni echoed in awed agreement.

I could almost picture the still-faceless Brianna rolling her eyes and the thought makes me grin.

"Well, you're honest," I said. "That's a plus. How about you Brianna?"

I actually was looking forward to hearing what might come out of her mouth and I have no idea why other than that this show has simultaneously screwed with my head and taken my will to live. "Why should I make you my wife, doll?"

"Honestly...you probably shouldn't."

Hold the fuck up—*what?*

I couldn't hold back my low rumbling laughter.

"Are you kidding me right now?"

This girl has done nothing but make me laugh and I couldn't wait anymore. I was done. I stood and went over to the wall then knocked on it.

"Alright, let me out," I said, causing a roar of applause from the small audience they had brought in. "I gotta meet this woman."

The show's host laughed his way through telling me that I had to wait just a little longer.

It's funny how closing your eyes can make you see someone you might have never looked at.

"Did you seriously just tell me not to marry you?" I asked, laughing as I returned to my chair. "Isn't that the entire point of being on this show?"

It didn't escape me how easily my words were now coming out.

She made it feel like the world wasn't watching and it was just me and her messing around like old friends.

"Well, I thought it was going to be a trivia show," she explained, snickering. "When I met my competition I was like; how hard can these questions really be? Am I right, Tiff?" I could almost hear the scowl on Tiffinni's face. "When you asked us what our favorite numbers were, I was like; *I got this!* Then these two went and snatched my answer right out from under me so I had to scramble to think of something on the fly."

I was laughing my ass off, squeezing my eyes shut to keep the tears from falling. I could hear the people in my ear piece in full-on fucking hysterics.

"Time," the voice in my earpiece choked on his laugh.

"Okay, okay, stop." I panted as I wiped away the wet from under my eyes. "Okay, seriously. Give me your best answer, baby. Why should I pick you to be my wife?"

She deadpanned, "Because we're clearly soul mates."

No matter what the hell this girl ended up looking like, I just wanted to wrap my arms around her and thank her for making me feel like I wasn't alone in this nightmare.

Bachelorette number three wasn't really trying to drag my ass to the altar. Even though she had been joking around about it, I still got the feeling that she never wanted to be a part of this shitshow. But then hell—*neither did I.*

"Mystery bachelor," The host said. "Have you made your final choice?"

"Yeah, I have." And I want out of this fucking box so I can see what she looks like. "I'm choosing Brianna."

"Word," the guy in my ear piece says. "I'd tap Brie's fine ass in a heartbeat."

I fucking knew ear-piece guy was holding out on me.

"Fuck," I whisper to myself anxiously, my pulse racing the same way it does right before I go on stage.

"Ladies and gentlemen—are you ready to meet our celebrity bachelor?" The audience replies with a crazy amount of applause. "Then let's bring him out!"

I stood when they cued up a clip of one of my band's most popular songs and I pulled the ear piece out of my ear, dropping it on my chair like I had been instructed to do.

At the same time, the plexiglass walls began to fall down around me and I stood in the middle of the chaos, stunned, because I thought they were just going to open up a fucking door or something—not drop the set on me.

The minute my mind cleared, my eyes found the women.

All three of them are fucking beautiful, but one of them

was very different from the others and my eyes locked on her.

"Oh my God!" One of the other two women shrieked, followed by the other. "It's Trax Thomas!"

I grimaced as the two of them came running over to me. Four arms wrapped around me like needy boa constrictors.

"Alright, alright," I soothed them both quietly, trying to ease them off of me. I was well-versed in the art of peeling overzealous fans off of my body.

My eyes were glued on the third woman.

Brianna.

She was still sitting in her chair, her pretty eyes rolling at me and making me grin.

Either she didn't know who I was, which was pretty unlikely, or she just didn't give a shit.

That thought was all it took to make me crave her approval like a fucking insecure teenage boy.

She was going to give a shit by the time I was done with her.

I eased the other girls aside and began walking toward her on a mission, like she was a magnet and I was made of metal.

When she saw the determination in my eyes, she jumped from her chair and began to scurry away from me. I grabbed her up from behind and twirled her tiny body in a tight embrace.

"Tell me I got the right person," I murmured in her ear, still holding her as the audience laughed and applauded.

Her unique fragrance hinted of hazelnut coffee and made me inhale her smell even deeper, committing it to memory.

"Who is it that you're looking for?" She asked over her shoulder, her voice giving her away.

"My soul mate." I rumbled a deep laugh in her ear and planting a hard kiss on her cheek before I finally let her go. "You're a fucking trip, you know that?"

"Wasn't trying to be," she said, flicking her playful eyes up to mine.

"I know." I gave her a wink before I pulled her by the hand toward the host to give our exit interviews. For some reason, I couldn't let go. And for some reason, she didn't make me.

My eyes kept pulling back to Brianna's face. She was young and fucking gorgeous; glowing with the kind of beauty that will still shine through when she's old.

She oozed with the kind of self assurance that told me she would never be used as a rag to shine anyone else up. She was witty, snarky, intelligent and so…exactly the kind of woman that would have been on the list if I had filled it out myself.

She smiled up at me when she caught me looking at her, but I didn't get the sense that she was flirting—just happy.

Something inside me told me that I needed to get to know this woman better—that she'd be good for my sorry ass.

And hell—maybe I'd be good for hers, too.

Brianna

At first, I was a little upset that Trax had chosen me.

But it was a blind round, so I really couldn't blame him for choosing my elegantly worded fluff over the cotton candy responses of the other two. In a way, some part of me even felt like his choice had redeemed rock stars everywhere.

The next competition round would be based solely on looks, and with perfect tens like Buffy and Fluffy on the menu, my perfect six self would be off the hook.

After filming was over and the set had cleared of everyone but the set crew, I began working on the clean-up tasks I would have been doing that night.

As impractical as my outfit was to work in, I hadn't wanted to waste any time changing out of the skirt and boots, and got straight to work.

Wrapping a power cord around my elbow and hand, I noticed Austin slowly walking toward me with an expression that told me he wasn't happy about what he was going to say.

My heart clutched, worrying that I had disappointed or upset him with my behavior on-camera.

I hadn't been thinking—I had been reacting; and my instincts ended up leading me in the wrong direction.

Unfortunately for me, this meant that I ended up coming across as *myself* on camera.

I mentally slapped myself.

I should have given him cotton candy responses.

In my attempt to be off-putting, I stood out as different, and people who don't like making choices make the most obvious ones.

Austin's hands were shoved into his front pockets and his face was a mask, as it usually was.

I felt like shrinking into the shadows.

"Brianna—a word…*privately*?"

His voice was calm, considering my own nerves were creating enough friction to heat an entire shopping mall.

My thoughts began spiraling.

I couldn't afford to get fired over this.

I needed these internship credits for my degree. I had less than two weeks left!

Getting fired would set me back an entire semester.

I'd have to write a letter to my benefactor explaining why I got fired, and they would probably be so disgusted that they'd retract all of my previous tuition payments—it would cost me everything!

Why hadn't I just played by the rules?

Why hadn't I just sat there and giggled like an airhead and answered 69 and just…not been stupid enough to lose my internship?

It's not like it even made a difference—he still chose me.

My face flushed with warmth and I swallowed hard, setting the cord down before following him across the set in the direction of the funeral for all of my hopes and dreams.

I mentally slapped myself just before he finally turned to face me.

"He's chosen you."

His words were flat, his eyes steady on mine as he stood

with folded arms.

I nodded.

We stood like that in silence for so uncomfortably long that I had to avert my eyes.

"You understand that was not part of our plan, correct?"

Our plan? There was a plan?

While I was slightly confused by this accusation, I only nodded.

I just couldn't hold the intensity of his gaze any longer and looked everywhere but at him.

He curled his fingertips gently beneath my chin, sending a wave of desire through my entire body.

I lifted my eyes to his.

"You are incredible in front of the camera, Brianna." Something akin to jealousy burned behind his expression. "Don't be."

He withdrew his hand and I missed the contact immediately.

"We're going to have a meeting to go over the show's initial ratings and viewer feedback first thing tomorrow morning. Will you be able to join us?"

I shook my head. "I'm sorry, I have to work at the coffee shop from 5 until 1."

"I sometimes forget..."

His heated gaze travelled slowly over my body in a way that would have made me uncomfortable, had I not been so incredibly attracted to him.

He looked off to the side and pulled his lower lip between his teeth before turning his eyes back to mine. "Would you want to get a drink with me later?"

His expressive eyes didn't tell me that it was *drinks* he was asking for.

My mouth fell open slightly, unprepared for the question.

How could I *refuse* this man and still keep my job?

Conversely, how could I *accept* his offer and still keep my job?

Fired for rejecting my boss or fired for having sex with him?

Rejection? *Sex*. Rejection? *Sex*.

"I, uh…" He must have read my face because the rejection in his eyes began to seep through his carefully practiced mask. Part of my heart died.

"I'd love to have drinks with you. Just…*after* my internship is over, if you don't mind."

He smiled, almost sadly, "Of course."

Trax

My soul mate, as she had referred to herself, was leaning over the vanity in her dressing room with her short hair pulled back into a headband. She scrubbed at her face with a wash cloth as she grumbled out loud to herself.

"Gah! I hate makeup!"

I leaned against the door frame with my arms folded over my chest, admiring her ass for another minute or so before I cleared my throat.

She glanced up at my reflection in her mirror and to my surprise she didn't flinch or try to hide the fact that she looked pretty unbecoming in the moment.

This girl really could give a shit what I thought about her.

"Oh, hey," she said, treating me like I was just any old person and not a fucking music icon, like everyone else on the whole goddamned planet. "Sorry I was a bit abrasive out there. I was coerced into being on the show at the last minute and I wasn't really prepared for it."

"Ditto," I replied. "And for the record, I didn't think you were abrasive."

She began rubbing white stuff on her cheeks, basically ignoring the fact that I was still standing there in her doorway.

"Mind if I join you?" I asked, flinging my hand in the direction of the couch.

"Sure," she shrugged.

I wandered over and flopped back into it, stretching my arms over the back as I propped a foot on my knee and continued to stare unabashedly at her perfect ass in skinny jeans.

"You can call me Kevin, by the way."

I felt myself slipping into the awkward person I became when the spotlight was off of me.

What the fuck was I even doing? I had no idea what I wanted to say to her. I honestly just wanted to stare at her for a while without saying shit.

She smirked at me like I was a complete dumbass, but she didn't say anything.

"You go by Brianna then?"

Fuck. *Why does making small talk have to be so damn hard?*

"People I'm close to call me Brie, but most people don't."

"So what's your main gig, Brie?" I asked, making it clear that I wasn't going to let her lump me in with *most people.*

"My gig…" She repeated, the smile in her voice making me smile without even seeing her face. "…as glamorous as it is, is a full-time barista. I've been working on my masters in video production and I intern about sixteen hours a week here at the studio."

I leaned forward, resting my elbows on my knees and began twirling the ring on my thumb.

"You ever heard of my band? Chevron Dreams?"

If she says no she's a fucking liar.

"I have," she admits. "But I'm honestly not very familiar with your music."

"You don't listen to the radio?" I raise my eyebrows skeptically. "War Torn? Shades of Red? Bring it Back?"

"Sorry," she shrugged. "The coffee shop where I work has a classical music only policy and I don't really listen to much music outside of work. I prefer the quiet, at home."

I turned my head and stared out the window beside me, running my hand over my stubbled face. I felt myself chuckling and knew it was in response to the sensation bubbling up inside of my chest. This girl was a blank slate I could write whatever I wanted on—a fucking anomaly—and damn, did I want to tattoo my graffiti all over her.

No wonder she doesn't give a shit about who I am—to her; I'm *nothing*.

I turned back to look at her again.

She had taken off the headband and when she turned toward me my breath caught in my goddamn lungs.

All that studio makeup had been hiding a face full of freckles.

I casually grabbed a throw pillow and held it in my lap.

"So…" I began, clearing the embarrassment from my throat. "Guess we're supposed to be going out on a date this week."

A date that I was now looking so damn forward to it physically ached.

"Yeah, about that," she said. "I know you're supposed to plan it as a surprise, but would you mind keeping it kind of simple? Nothing sappy or romantic."

"You don't like sappy and romantic?"

"In a normal situation, maybe. But this whole thing…" she waved her hand around. "It's all just fake."

"Fake," I repeated, nodding like I agreed with her.

Completely fake. Nothing to see here. Just a guy with a pillow in his lap for no good reason and a chick that says every damn thing a guy like me should want to hear.

"I mean, neither of us are really trying to make an actual connection here." She squinted at me curiously; probably because I was gazing at her like a fucking idiot. "Right?"

"Uh huh," I replied, still mesmerized by her freckles—just enough to be beautiful, but not so many that they take away from her amazing eyes.

"Go easy on me this week, then next week you can lay it on thick with one of the other girls and the viewers will go nuts over it."

I felt blindsided.

Other girls? Viewers?

No.

Fuck no.

This was her polite way of rejecting me.

"What makes you think I'm going to pick one of them next week?" I ask, almost defensively.

"Well, I just figured…" She seemed genuinely confused, "I mean…you do understand that you can't pick me three times, right?"

"Uh, why not?"

"Because if you do it will contractually obligate the two of us to get married!"

I held my arms out wide, argumentatively, "Isn't that the whole point of this?"

"The point of this," she says, twirling her finger around calmly as she perched on the arm of the couch, "Is for you to gain publicity for your band. Not to end up married to a complete stranger."

"You see, that's where you're wrong," I grinned at her smugly. "I don't feel like we're complete strangers anymore."

She quirked an eyebrow at me and folded her arms over her chest. "Really."

I chuckled at her response at the same time I got the strong urge to pull her under me and slide my tongue over her eyelids—a weird fucking first for me, but hey—why deny it?

She stood up and walked over to the vanity, grabbing her

purse and throwing the strap over her shoulder. "Well, since we're such close friends now, how about walking me to the Metro. It's getting dark."

"I'll do you one better." I stood and tossed the pillow onto the couch. "I'll drive you home."

Pulling up to the curb in front of her apartment building, she turned to me, "Can I give you some gas money or something?"

"Nah, we're good."

"Alright, well, thanks for the ride. I guess I'll see you on our date."

"Unless you want to invite me up," I grinned at her playfully.

She laughed, slamming an invisible dent into my ego.

"Maybe some other time," she said, patting my leg.

I grabbed her hand, intertwining our fingers. "Like after our second date?"

She pulled her hand from mine, "There won't be a second date. We already talked about this—remember?"

"Ah, but you're wrong," I pointed at her, smiling. "You said *three* dates were out of the question."

"Same difference."

"I don't think you understand the significance of the situation. A second date with me is an honor very few women get."

"Oh, well I'm *so* flattered," she rolled her eyes, unimpressed. "But you can go ahead and put that enormous ego back in your pants because a second date is not going to happen."

"The fuck it ain't," I laughed wholeheartedly. "I need more of you; one date isn't going to be enough for me."

She placed her hand flat against my chest to keep me at a distance, "We're going on one date, and only because I'm contractually obligated."

"Don't flirt with me like that," I said, slowly sliding my fingers over her wrist and leaning toward her. "I might just kiss you."

"Don't threaten me, rock star," she whispered, licking her lips as she stared back at me with half-lidded eyes before opening her door.

"Goodnight, Brie." I grinned, watching to make sure she made it into her building before pulling away from the curb.

There were a shit ton of people walking the streets in her part of Los Angeles at night. One of them looked too damn familiar to just be a coincidence but I shrugged it off as just that.

Brianna

"Oh my God, Brie! *Trax Thomas?*"

Gabby squealed at me the minute I walked through the door the next morning. Between her reaction and all of the strange looks I had gotten on the Metro on the way in, I figured the first episode had aired without a hitch.

I had been too mortified to watch the replay after I got home, and I had been intentionally avoiding social media all morning. On a quick glance, I noticed I had over two-thousand new friend requests already bombarding one of my accounts.

It wasn't the friend requests I was trying to avoid—it was the haters.

All it would take is one hateful comment to put my mind in a place I wasn't ready or willing to go that morning.

"He's like as hot as…" Gabby gushed like a crazed fan. "…as…*No!*" I raised an eyebrow at her, seeing where she was going with this. "There is no comparing his hotness to anyone. He's at the very top of the hottie chart. He's completely undefeated."

"He is pretty hot," I replied with very little emotion as I grabbed a new cash drawer from the safe and popped it into the register, signing on for my shift. "He's actually pretty nice, too."

"So, why aren't you freaking out?" She demands.

I pulled my apron over my head.

"Believe me, I'm freaking out. But not over him."

Her eyes went all dreamy and she sighed. "Ugh! I just want to run my fingers through those long brown curls of his and tie myself to him."

I scrunched my nose at her. "Yeah, that's not weird or anything."

"He's just so…*yum*."

"Right," I rolled my eyes, making us both chuckle.

"So when do you go on your date?" She asked eagerly.

"Sometime this week," I replied. "The studio will contact me."

"The studio? You mean you don't have his cell number?"

"Yeah, right." I snorted, "It's not a real date, Gab."

The bells on the front door chimed and our bakery delivery guy pulled his hand truck in.

"Well, look who's here," Tyrone teased. "If it ain't the infamous grunge queen."

I rolled my eyes at him, "Very funny, Ty."

"Can you believe Brie's going to marry Trax Thomas?" Gabby squealed.

"Would you stop saying that?"

Tyrone gave me that cool, half-lidded gaze of his, and the two of them stood side-by-side grinning at me in very different ways.

"Ugh! Gabby, just get the coffee going. Ty, don't you have any other deliveries to make this morning?"

He began unloading racks of bagels and pastries onto the bakery shelves.

"Mm hm," he mumbled. "Whatever you say, bridezilla."

"Oh my gosh!" Gabby suddenly exclaimed, spinning to

face me, her eyes wide with realization. "Oh my gosh, Brie! If you marry him, you'll get to," her voice lowered to an envious hiss, "sleep with him."

Tyrone's belly laugh was infectious, making it hard to restrain my own laughter.

"I don't know, Boo, you might want to make sure that guy gets tested first. Them rock stars—they into some nasty shit. Threesomes…foursomes…"

"Ew! Stop it!" I laughed, nearly coughing to death. "I am not sleeping with him. Or marrying him. Or filing joint tax returns with him. It's just a show."

The front door opened again and a man holding a bouquet of flowers came in, "Delivery for a Miss Brianna Rose?"

Gabby and Tyrone looked at each other with knowing grins and I shot a glare toward them.

"I'm Brianna Rose," I replied, accepting the flowers from him. "Thank you."

After the man left, I pulled the little card from the bouquet and shrugged away from Gabby, who was peeking over my shoulder.

Thank you for all you do.
Happily indebted to you,
Austin

"Happily indebted to you…*Austin*?" Gabby read the card and lifted her eyes to me. "Isn't he the hottie who got you the internship?"

I held my palms up, squeezing my lips shut.

"Oh my gosh!" Her eyes widened with her grin, "You're screwing your boss?"

"No, I am not!" I virtually scream. "He…he asked me out. I told him no. For now."

"For now? No wonder you're not freaking out about Trax!

You've got hottie millionaires lining up around the block for you!"

"I do not!"

Tyrone pushed his cart toward the door, slapping me on the back as he passed, "Good luck with all that, Miss Brie, but you're better off with a normal guy like me."

"Ooh, is that an offer?" Gabby asked on my behalf, wiggling her eyebrows.

"Yeah, right," he replied, waving her off. "Brie's sweet and all, but I don't date the ladies on my route. It's bad for business."

A customer slipped in past Tyrone, and I shoved Gabby gently behind the counter.

"Open for business," I murmured quietly at her, "Which means mouths are closed."

The customer made her way to the counter, "I'd like a tall hot coffee with two pumps of vanilla; take-out please."

I entered her order on the screen, "Your total is five-nineteen."

She handed me a ten dollar bill and as I made change for her, I noticed her eyeing me curiously. Finally she decided to voice what she had been thinking.

"This is kind of a strange question, but were you the girl on *Mistery Marriage* last night?"

Considering the town we were in, it wasn't really all that strange of a question. We were on the outskirts of Hollywood—seeing people who are on television isn't all that unusual.

I opened my mouth to answer but Gabby chimed in behind me, slowly sliding the lady's coffee across the counter toward her with a huge grin, "Yes, that was her."

I handed the lady her change, humbly nodding.

The lady stuffed a dollar bill into the tip jar on the counter.

"You were absolutely hilarious! Good luck!"

"Thanks," I replied as she took her coffee and left.

I let out a sigh and turned to glare at Gabby, "Please don't encourage them."

"Just think of me as the first member of your fan club."

Austin

Every ounce of reason had left me when I sent Brianna those flowers.

I had called the flower shop an hour later to retract the order, but they had already delivered them.

I stared straight through the stack of papers on my desk, unable to quiet the feelings churning around inside me.

Jealousy.

It wasn't a feeling I often felt, but I recognized the burn of it. The way her skirt flirted with the back of her thighs broke me into a thousand pieces, every one of them lying beneath her feet.

I was envious of Kevin Thomas.

And I was furious with myself.

I had carelessly used her as a shield for my own failure, virtually throwing her into his path. I asked her out because I was jealous. I offered her myself so that she would not become invested in the idea of him. Yes, I wanted her—*God, I wanted her*—but it wasn't the time.

Every date I had ever gone on had been an uncomplicated matter. A simple transaction, wherein at the end of the night the transaction was finalized and that was the end of it.

But Brianna was an utter complication. There was no *end of the night* with her.

She was the grand finalé.

A flame burning on the ice.

So beautiful, yet so much more dangerous the closer I approached.

I blew out a long breath.

The thought of him pursuing her beyond the walls of this set made my head begin to throb.

I had no doubt she would only be a pebble in his bucket of sexual conquests, but to me she was everything innocent and beautiful there was to be found in this life.

The moment I first saw her smile at me, I knew she would be mine. *I've made sure of it.*

Trax

I was exhausted and hungover and I still got up early to go to the damn meeting at the studio just so I could see her again. There was no way in hell the girl was as perfect as I was remembering her so I wanted to prove it to myself, but then she never fucking showed up.

After listening to a bunch of bullshit about reviews and viewer ratings, I ended up falling asleep outside of Austin's office, waiting to talk with him and Heath about the date I was supposed to be planning.

After leaving the studio the night before, I had ended up in this dive bar with a bunch of Chevron fans who were watching a replay of the show. It was a fucking trip to hear their reactions before they realized who was sitting right there at the bar with them.

None of the reviews from this morning's meeting meant shit to me.

It was hearing it right from the mouths of my own fans that I cared about.

The consensus in that bar was that people wanted me to come out of the show the same single, man-whoring rocker I always was. It felt like a kick in the nuts, because all it told me was that none of my fans really knew a damn thing more about me than what the media spun to them.

It was my own fault for always letting other people speak for me, and that was something I was now committing myself to change. It was time to start aligning who I really am with who the world perceives me to be.

Enter Brianna.

She ain't bad to look at, and she's cool as hell to be around. If I could somehow pull off this PR gig and score myself a sweet little woman, it could be a solid opening for my image revamp: Trax Thomas—*family man*.

Ever since my mom died, I'd been kicking around the idea that maybe I was ready to give up the bachelor life. I'd spent the past fifteen years of my life out on the road, and despite the insane number of people who were constantly around me, I was just fucking lonely.

I wasn't interested in hooking up with random chicks anymore, and I even caught myself envying Zach whenever he visited with his kid, wondering what it would like to be a dad.

Fans have expectations for me that don't apply to the other guys in the band because I'm the face out front, the voice—*the god of grunge*—and sometimes I just fucking hate being in that box they put me in.

Maybe this show was meant to be a wake-up call for me. A kick in the right direction.

As Heath and I went over the date I had planned for Brie, Austin just sat there glaring at his desk. I got the distinct impression that he was pissed about something I said so I crossed my arms over my chest and peered at him. "Why aren't you saying anything?"

"The hot tub is too much." He dropped his pen and steepled his fingers.

Heath sighed, rolling his eyes, "They'll be wearing bathing suits."

Austin ticked his jaw. "It's intimate. It's sexual. And it is not appropriate for this show."

"Look," I say, flinging my arms out. "I have to do what my fans expect, and what they expect is a sexy little make-out sesh in the hot tub."

"Absolutely not!" He barked out through his teeth, giving me a way more heated response than I had provoked. "Not on my show. Not with Brianna. Not at all."

Not with Brianna. *Interesting.*

"So what happens if I marry her?" I bite back, intentionally pushing his buttons to test a theory. "Would it be a strictly platonic marriage? Is there some hidden clause in the contract that says I'm not allowed to fuck my own wife?"

His eye twitched as he glared at me, giving me all the evidence I needed.

"She's not your wife and I highly doubt that anyone will be getting married," Austin tried to cool his anger as he gathered his paperwork. "Your PR manager made it quite clear where you stand on the idea of marriage."

"He did?" I lifted an eyebrow, leaning my hip against the table. "Enlighten me."

He tapped his papers in a neat little stack and said, "That will be unnecessary."

"Oh, I think it's necessary. I want to clear this up right now. Do you have a problem with me marrying one of your contestants?" I didn't outright say Brianna, but he knew exactly who I meant.

"Mr. Thomas, you have a contract with our studio that both entitles and requires you to see this through to the end of the eighth episode, regardless of the outcome. If you decide to marry any of the contenders, it will be a legally binding marriage in the state of California. All prenuptial agreements and other matters of that kind will be taken care of by our legal teams and you and your assets will be thoroughly protected." He lifted his eyes to me. "Our studio can provide you or your lawyers with a clean background check for each woman which can also, upon your request, include a full sexual health screening. We can not, however, view or share with you the results. That being said, if you choose to sleep with any of these women," he narrowed his eyes, making a very clear threat, "you do so at your own risk."

I grunted out a laugh, shaking my head. "Beautiful."

"This studio stands behind our contracts. Once the final episode is released, all responsibility for divorce, as well as any resulting negative publicity, is no longer ours. So long as your behavior does not reflect negatively upon our studio, you are free to do as you wish. But I suggest you consider your path going forward very carefully before making any life-altering decisions."

"You sound like you're trying to talk me out of the exact same thing your company tried to talk me into a few weeks ago."

"Heath," Austin turned to the man. "Could you please excuse us for a moment?"

Heath left the room, glancing my way before pulling the door shut behind him.

Austin turned back to me, "May I be candid with you?"

I nodded, "Shoot."

"I get the impression that you're already favoring Brianna over the other two ladies."

I shrugged.

"I think you should be aware of the fact that she was not originally chosen to be one of the contestants. Our third contestant left us in the lurch at the eleventh hour so we had to find a substitute in order to proceed with filming."

"And?"

"And Brianna has absolutely no interest in leaving this show with a husband."

"And I had absolutely no interest in leaving this show with a wife. But things change. If Brie signed the same contract we all did, that means she's contractually obligated to marry me *if I say so*." Austin looked at the wall behind me, trying not to let his frustration show any more than it already has. "Your studio is contractually obligated to provide me with the wife of my choosing based upon the rules of the show. Am I correct?"

He swallowed hard, anger brewing in his glare. "Yes."

"Well, there you have it," I turned toward the door and opened it.

"Wait," his voice was broken.

I froze with my hands pressed against both door jambs, but I didn't turn back to look at him.

"I made a mistake in asking Brianna to be a part of this show. I regret that decision in a way you cannot possibly understand. Name your price and I will pay it out of my own pocket, just please…do not pursue her any further."

Shit.

The fucker's in love with her.

I looked down at the ground and thought of that freckled face and playful smile. I had just met Brie so there was no way of knowing how this would play out between us, but the woman had gained my undivided attention in less than a day and nobody had done that in…well, shit—ever.

Name my price.

I shook my head in a non-answer right before I walked out.

Brianna

"Girl, don't make me tie you to that chair. Just sit your ass down and let me do my job."

I scrunched my nose as Wanda powdered it.

"Do you really have to use all that makeup?"

"Do you have any idea what those freckles will end up looking like on a high-def TV? I promise you—you will thank me."

I squinted at myself in the mirror as she hid the only thing that made me recognize myself in my reflection.

"So word around town is Austin asked you out," she says, just as casually as she would ask me how I like the weather in California.

My eyes darted to her reflection in the mirror.

"Where did you hear that?"

"You were still wired up. Paxson overheard the whole thing through your mic."

"Shit," I said, feeling the burn of humiliation on the back of my neck.

"Don't worry," she said. "I ain't said nothing to nobody. I may give you shit about it, but I ain't crazy enough to put my job on the line by spreading gossip."

"Is Paxson?" I asked nervously.

"Oh, hell no," she said with a dismissive wave of her hand. "Only reason I know is because we've been hooking up for the past year. We talk shit about everyone when we're at home, you know how it is."

I sighed.

"So you told him no, huh?" She pried, pushing at my shoulder playfully.

I nodded and she let out a howl of laughter with a clap of her hands. "Good for you! It's the chase them rich boys want. The minute they get what they're after, they'll drop your ass down in Compton with a map and a flashlight."

"What?"

She waved her hand, "Forget it. That's a story for another day."

I stared at myself for a while as she moved to working on my hair. I was a far cry from the girl in lime boots. She and Fabiano had made me up with the whole "farmer's daughter" look. And when I was escorted to the limo for my date, I was met with a stunned gaze.

Trax

One camera followed Brie from the front door of the studio while another was on me as I stood by the limo. Someday when I'm looking back and remembering some of the most defining moments of my life, I'm going to be able to push rewind on that shit and watch it again and again.

Over the past fifteen years, I've been in the presence of thousands of beautiful women; models, dancers, actresses—hell, even a princess or two. But not one of them ever made me feel the way this one did the moment I saw her walk out of that studio.

I honestly couldn't tell you what it was about her. I barely knew shit about the girl, but for some reason just the idea of seeing her gave me those same crazy carbonated feelings of excitement in the pit of my stomach I used to get as a kid the night before Santa came.

It was the first time I had seen her since dropping her off in front of her apartment and I'd be lying if I said I hadn't thought about going back a time or two.

I wasn't desperate or deprived.

All I'd have to do is stand on the fucking sidewalk and beautiful women would show up, eager to offer me a good time. Makes me sound like a cocky son of a bitch, and maybe I am one, but that doesn't make it any less true.

The thing is, when women come easy, you find less and less reason to want them around.

I lost my taste for groupies a long time ago but had kept it up until about a year ago because it was what I was expected to do. In this past year I've done a lot of growing up and growing out of my image.

I look at Brianna and notice how calm she is.

How completely disinterested she is in me, and that only makes me want to win her over so much more.

I don't want to be insignificant to this woman.

I don't want to be part of a role she's playing right now and that's exactly what I am to her.

For a man who prefers to live in the shadows of his own fame, I fucking want to shine right now, just so she'll see me.

I held out my hand to help her into the back of the limo. Her tiny hand fits in mine like it was made just for me to hold it and its hard to let go.

I close the door for her and begin my walk around to the other side.

How would my fans perception of me change if they knew what was going on inside of me right now? How would they feel if they knew I would give just about anything for that sweet little thing in the car to just want me? A woman I have known for less than a full three hours of my life?

Would they stop listening to my music? Think I was pathetic and desperate? 'Cause I sure as hell do, but again—that doesn't make it any less true.

I ran my hand over my face.

Rock Gods Don't Fall in Love.

They don't have wives—they have fans.

My fans have given me hundreds of millions of their dollars on the unwritten understanding that my bachelor image is part of the package. Musicians are servants to the people with the money, so we must give them what they are buying.

Family changes a man.

It changes his music.

I open the door and climb into the limo, sliding all the way across the seat so our legs are pressed together. I slip my hand to the inside of her thigh, possessively and gaze into her eyes.

This woman right here? She's a tempting, poisonous fruit with the power to fuck up my entire existence.

Despite the cameras pointing at us from three angles in the limo, I lean over and try to taste her poison.

Austin

The loud crack of my pencil snapping in half only draws attention from Heath.

"Did he really just try to kiss her?" Tilly laughs. "The date hasn't even started yet!"

A low growl escaped me.

Why was I tormenting myself, watching their date through the editing screens?

Knowing this was my own doing made my anger even worse and I felt like reigning fire upon the entire fucking world.

"Damn, that guy is smooth," the film editor joked. "She's going to be eating out of his hands by the end of the night."

"No way. Don't you notice how she keeps moving farther away from him?" Tilly said, pointing to the screen. "She's already slid away from him three times and totally blew off that kiss."

My eyes settle on the screen focused on Brianna's face.

She's absolutely breathtaking.

Ghosts of my fingers stroke her cheek upon the screen as I clutch my hands into tight fists at my side. My eyes close as I imagine pressing my lips against hers, but instead of calming me as it should, my stomach begins to swirl with jealousy.

I'm not the one in that car with her.

I'm not there to make sure she is safe, protected, *still mine…*

It's more than I can bear to think that she could be seduced by this man and robbed of her innocence all because of me.

Me—damn it!

She won't even look at me, now—averting her eyes whenever we're in the same room.

She never mentioned the flowers and now something has changed between us.

She's pushing me away because I made the mistake of letting her know I was attracted to her.

All because I forced her into doing this show and *he* fucking fell for her when he wasn't supposed to!

All because I couldn't just fucking stay away from that coffee shop—away from her!

I couldn't just leave her alone!

Now she knows me, despises me, damns me to this suffering…

Now she'll never unlock that goddamned door!

The snake that was coiling in my gut was growing impatient with being held back.

"Did you see that?" Tilly's laughter was grating…louder… I felt my body trembling. "He tried to hold her hand but she just casually slid it right back out of his. She must have worked with egotistical celebrities before."

"No, she hasn't," I mumbled before I realized I had even opened my mouth. Three sets of curious eyes turned to look at me. "It's my job to know the work experience of all my interns."

"Is that so?" Heath grinned. "What field does Onja major in?"

"Who the hell is Onja?" I asked.

"One of your interns," Tilly replied, lifting a glass of wine in my direction and toasting me with hers. I snatched the glass out of her hand and swallow it in one go.

Brianna

"It was an actual, literal nightmare," I said, talking to Gabby between customers.

"Like a spooky skeletons and ghosts, level nightmare?" Gabby clarified.

"Like an 'Edvard Munch hold your face and scream' level nightmare."

Until it wasn't.

Until the cameras stopped rolling and we sat in the hot tub together for hours after the camera crews left, just talking and learning about each other.

"You look unhappy," Kevin had said as he tilted his head back and looked up at the stars.

He stretched his arms out across the back of the hot tub and rested a hand on my shoulder, giving it a playful scratch to get my attention.

At my height, my sore body was mostly submerged beneath the warm water, and I sat gliding my arms back and forth just under the surface in a calming motion.

"I'm not unhappy," I replied, "I'm just recovering from our date."

A deep chuckle rumbled from his chest, "Sorry about that."

I shrugged, "I'll live. And to be fair, it was kind of fun."

I felt him watching me for a long while before he spoke again.

"You're a very unusual woman, you know that?"

I looked over at him, "What do you mean?"

He chuckled, shaking his head, "Here we are all alone in a hot tub, camera crews are gone…and you're still sitting so far away from me the water is actually getting colder."

"There's only one reason the water would be getting warmer if I moved closer." I scrunched my nose playfully at him. "You sure you want that?"

"There's another first for me." He laughed outright. "I've never been in a hot tub with a woman who threatened to piss in it."

I cackled, making him laugh even harder.

"Are you saying you haven't been in a hot tub with someone as immature as me?"

"Maybe not. How old are you anyway?"

"17," I replied, watching his eyes grow and muscles stiffen simultaneously as I fought back my smile.

"Are you fucking with me?" He asked in a deadly serious voice.

I let out my laughter "I'm 23!"

He exhaled loudly, "Fuck, Brie! That shit isn't funny! I thought you were serious!"

"I don't look 17," I protest with a giggle.

"You also don't look anywhere near my age," he replied, still recovering.

"Yeah, there's no way in hell I look fifty."

"Fuck you, I'm 35," he splashed me.

The water finally calmed and we both sat quiet until he reached over and grabbed me by the waist, pulling me onto his lap and keeping his arms looped around me.

We sat like that for a long time in silence, just listening to the sound of the bubbling water jets.

"So what's the deal with Austin?" He finally asked. "Are you two hooking up?"

"No," I shook my head in confusion. "Why would you think that?"

"I just had a feeling there was something more going on there."

I wanted to press for more, but decided it was better to just let it go.

He began to slide his fingers back and forth over my stomach, making goosebumps rise up on my skin.

"So tell me more about yourself, bachelorette number three," he murmured into my ear, resting his scratchy chin on my shoulder.

"There isn't much to tell." I stare at the glide of my hands beneath the surface of the water. "I'm actually a pretty boring person."

"Then I want to know every boring detail about you," he said.

"Why?" I asked, turning to meet his eyes.

"Because you interest me," he stared at the chain around my neck, sliding the charm to the front with the gentle glide of his fingertips across my skin.

I felt myself blush.

"How did you end up on the show?"

"Austin guilted me and honestly, I really needed the money."

"Yeah, I get that." He says.

"Fortunately, my tuition's already been paid. Someone really liked a video I made a few years ago and donated the money for my tuition. I just have to cover my living expenses, which hasn't been easy with the internship cutting into my hours."

His fingers suddenly stopped moving and I turned my face

to him. His eyes darted back and forth between mine quickly, searching for something I'm not sure he ever found.

"Hmm," he said oddly, then very slowly began moving his thumb in circles on my waist with just enough pressure to give me butterflies.

"You ever been married before, Brie?"

The silence that followed made me uncomfortable, "That's kind of a random question."

He shrugged, "Just figured we should get to know some shit about each other."

"Why? Have you?" I turned his question back on him.

He shook his head, "Nope, you'll be the first."

He coaxed me to turn on his lap and straddle him. He slipped his hands around my back and clasped his fingers behind me as he stared into my eyes. I slid my hands from his shoulders down to his muscular chest.

"What would you gain from marrying me?" I whispered nervously, finding myself being drawn into his gaze.

"A beautiful wife," he said, moving his forehead against mine as he pulled me closer. "Someone who makes me laugh." Eyes lidded, he smiled against my lips, trying to tempt me. "Cameras are gone, Brie…no reason to be shy if you want to take me for a test drive."

I so very badly wanted to kiss him, but I couldn't.

"Kevin," I said in a breathy voice, letting out a seductive little whimper before lifting my eyes to his. "I have to pee."

"Get the fuck off me!" He shoved me away with a laugh, causing me to plunge beneath the water. Still laughing, I reached over the edge of the tub and grabbed my towel, wrapping it around myself.

"You're beating the hell out of my ego," he laughed, standing up to help me climb out before he grabbed his towel. "That was my best pickup line!"

"You write lyrics for a living, and *that* was your best

pickup line?" I laughed.

"What? I'm not used to having to work so damn hard to get a woman's attention."

"I can imagine," I rolled my eyes.

"You just wait..." He climbed out of the tub and pushed a finger into my shoulder, "One of these days I'm going to figure out what makes you tick, and when I do, I won't show you any mercy."

I eased his finger away and he grinned down at me, "You're too fucking adorable."

I pushed into the house, "You're a pain in the ass."

Trax

"Yo, Freddy, we need to talk. Call me back"

I ended the message and shoved my phone back into the pocket of my jeans.

He ain't gonna call me back.

He thinks I'm pissed because of the show, but that ain't why I need to talk to him.

I sat on the edge of the hotel bed with my elbows propped on my knees and my fingertips steepled in front of me, staring at the patterns in the carpet.

What are the fucking chances that Brianna was the girl I had sponsored all those years ago?

Her story lines up, *mostly*.

I knew she wasn't bullshitting me tonight, either.

What I had done wasn't something anyone knew about other than Freddy, my accountants, and the school's financial aid director.

Brianna wouldn't have known who I was—it was all done anonymously. And I had no idea who she was because I wasn't a pompous asshole who went checking up on my investments. I didn't have time or interest in following through on the business end of shit—that's what I paid people for.

My mom had a story a lot like that girl in Brie's video, only when I found out my mom was being kicked out of her home I was fortunate enough to have the kind of money to prevent that shit from happening. Most people aren't lucky enough to have a son with the financial means to bail them out of medical debt. Not that she didn't put up a damn fight about it all the way to the fucking bank.

My mom didn't end up making it and that video landed in front of my eyes a few weeks after I lost her. It emotionally fucked me up—like *seriously* emotionally fucked me up.

I sent a shit-ton of money to a fund set up for the woman in the video, then I had Freddy find out who the videographer was—a sophomore at East Malvern.

Despite the protest of my accountants, I wanted to give her the kind of money that would allow her to be able to do what she did best; make life-changing videos. Ultimately we decided I would cover her and her husband's tuition and student loans then set them up with enough money for a studio.

The only reason Freddy was involved in the whole deal was because he had a contact in the video department of the college that could help make it happen.

It had to be her.

It fucking *had* to be her.

I mean, how often does this kind of shit happen for it to be a coincidence?

That video was still out there. All I had to do was one quick internet search and I'd have my answer.

Shit, if it was her…

I ran my hand over my face.

…shit.

The girl I had given all that money to was married.

Question is, is she *still* married?

She hadn't answered me when I asked her.

Did she get divorced and is opposed to marriage now? Is that why she's been so against marrying me?

She told me she was broke and working as a barista. I *gave* her the money for her own studio specifically to avoid that kind of shit. Why in the hell was she serving coffee instead of making life-changing films? What had she done with all the goddamn money?

I pulled out my phone and dialed again, punching my finger at the screen.

"Fucking call me, Freddy!"

Crazy shit was spiraling in my brain.

Fucking hell.

What if *Austin* was her husband?

What if he is *still* her husband?

Is Murray Studios the studio I funded for them?

What if I'm smack in the middle of a fucking Hollywood con job?

Fuck that—I'll marry that girl and get my money back out of her one slow and dirty fuck at a time. She's *my* fucking investment and I have a goddamned right to cash out!

I grabbed a pillow and threw it, trying to release some of the anger brewing inside me.

I flopped back on the bed and threw my forearm over my eyes, sighing loudly and trying to bring my pulse down.

I liked this chick.

I mean *really* liked her.

That's the whole damn problem.

No matter how much I try to convince myself she's been playing me, I know it ain't true.

She's not a con artist. There has to be something else going on that I can't see, and Freddy not calling me back is leaving me even more blind.

The way I see it, I got two choices; either ask Freddy, or get her to tell me herself.

And since Freddy ain't calling me back, it's all on me.

Brianna

I put the lid on a caramel macchiato and handed it to my customer, "Have a nice day!"

The early morning rush had passed and only a handful of regulars were still scattered around at tables, typing away on their phones and laptops.

I was exhausted after getting in so late, so I picked up a washcloth and began wandering the dining area, wiping off vacated seats and tabletops. Busy work. I tried to keep my mind from wandering back to that long conversation in the hot tub.

It was strange how comfortable I felt with Kevin.

I had honestly expected him to be arrogant or obnoxious, based on the way the media had always slanted his personality. But he was nothing at all like the man they painted him to be. He wasn't all leather and spikes—he was more like soft, warm flannel.

He loved to laugh, and for some strange reason he seemed to find me incredibly funny.

It would have been so easy to let myself fall under his spell last night, but after learning my lesson with Neil, I was now built with charm-resistant armor.

Coming back to the counter where Gabby was stacking napkins, I decided to continue where I had left off earlier that morning. "Can you believe he actually tried to kiss me on national television?"

"What I can't believe is that you didn't let him."

Gabby's disappointment in me was no big secret and she wasn't particularly shy about telling me exactly how she felt.

"Of course I didn't let him!" *No matter how much I might have wanted to.* "These videos are going to follow me around on the internet for the rest of my life. The last thing I need is for my future kids to stumble upon them and be like, 'Mom's kissing some guy on TV and it isn't Dad!"

She swatted me in the shoulder, "But he could be! He could be their dad!"

I laughed outright, "Not a chance in hell."

She stood with her arms crossed, giving me a disapproving look. "You didn't even give him a chance to be their dad. Those poor kids."

I heard the bells chime on the door and I began to move toward the register.

"I went on the date and now I'm off the hook." I saw Gabby's eyes grow wide as she stiffened, but I was too engrossed in my thoughts to pay any mind to another one of her anxiety attacks.

The sound of a man clearing his throat came from across the counter and I turned, feeling my eyes roll involuntarily.

Gabby pushed past me, extending her hand, "Hi, I'm Gabby. I'm a big fan."

"Pleasure to meet you, Gabby." Kevin fixed his eyes on me with a grin as he shook her hand.

"Shit." I mumble, looking around at all the eyes that were now on us—or more specifically; *him*. "What the hell are you doing here?"

Gabby shoved me, giving me a disapproving glare.

"I never got your number," he replied with twinkling eyes as he leaned casually on the counter.

Gabby stood beside me clutching a washcloth at her chest with one hand and fanning herself with the other.

"You don't need my number," I replied, curtly.

A prolonged squeak slipped out of Gabby's throat.

He chuckled at me through his gorgeous smile. "How else am I going to wear you down?"

I lowered my voice, "We'll probably get in really big trouble if the paparazzi finds out you're here. It will look like the entire show is fixed. Even worse, I'll start getting hounded relentlessly here at work. It's already starting on all my social media pages."

"Yeah, okay. I'll leave. I get it," He sighed, putting his sunglasses on. "But not unless you agree to go out with me tonight."

I shook my head, "A second date for us is not in the script."

He chuckled, leaning on the counter toward me, lowering his voice, "I'm talking about just you and me; no studio, no cameras, no contracts. Completely…" He slid his finger down my nose. "…*unscripted*." My toes curled inside of my shoes. "And just so we're clear; I'm going to pursue you relentlessly until you say yes."

"Why?" I whisper because my voice is hiding.

He lowered his voice and said, "Because I know what I want, Brie."

God, how I wished I could fall for this man, but it was impossible.

I shook my head, "I'm sorry, Kevin. I can't."

He looked at Gabby, who was mesmerized by him, "Is she always this stubborn?"

Gabby slowly shook her head, "No, it's definitely you."

"Then I guess I'm just going to have to try harder." He

handed Gabby his phone, "Put her number in."

Gabby began typing furiously with shaking hands as I glared at her. After she handed his phone back to him, he flashed us both a smile then turned and walked out the door.

I turned to Gabby, whose mouth still hung open as she stared after him.

"Are you crazy?" I shouted as quietly as possible.

She gripped me by my shoulders, gently shaking me."You do realize that he was talking about sex, right?"

"Of course I do!" I hissed.

The phone rang and I welcomed the chance to escape Gabby's eager opinion.

"Morning Glory Café, this is Brie, may I help you?"

"I'm beginning to lose my patience with you." A monotone masculine voice responds.

"What?" I ask, not entirely sure I had heard him correctly.

"I was watching you in the hot tub last night." The man's voice dropped to nearly a whisper, causing me to shiver. "Did you fuck him?"

My knees felt like jelly beneath me as prickles covered my neck. I began darting my eyes around the room nervously.

"Who is this?" I demand, hearing the trembling in my voice.

"You're mine, Brianna. And I don't like to share what's mine."

"Neil?"

"This is not. *Fucking. Neil!*" The man's voice strained, hissing Neil's name like it was a curse. As his voice grew angrier it took on an almost British accent. "If you don't want to find yourself tied to my bed you'd better stop sharing yours. Fuck him again and you'll be fucking a dead man."

The line went dead and my legs collapsed beneath me.

Austin tapped his pen furiously on the pad of paper on his

desk.

Even from my side of the desk I could tell he was bouncing his knee just as quickly.

He tossed the pen onto the pad and ran his hands over his pale and sweat glistened face before he took to tapping his thumb upon the desk, looking everywhere except into my eyes.

Withdrawing from the competition wasn't an option.

The money that I had already been paid would go a long way, but having all of it would provide me with enough money to be able to pack up and leave this town, *this state,* and live a comfortable life somewhere far less expensive.

"You shouldn't have stayed with him after the filming was done," he finally said. "I don't like that you were alone with him."

There was something odd about the tone of his voice. He wasn't scolding me, exactly—it was more like a warning.

The office door suddenly flew open and Kevin came in.

"Mr. Thomas," Austin held out a hand, motioning toward one of the chairs beside me. "Have a seat."

"What the fuck?" Kevin asked, looking over at me. "They told me someone threatened you?"

"And you," I nodded, pressing my fingers against my temples.

"Was it one of my fans?"

"No, I don't think so."

"Shit, Brie." He sighed. "I know it probably doesn't make you feel any better, but shit like this happens to me all the time. It's usually nothing to worry about."

"Whoever it was knew we were in the hot tub. Someone was watching us."

"Everyone who saw the show knew we were in a hot tub. I think someone is just trying to freak you out."

I could see Austin's fingers trembling, despite his efforts to hide them.

"Did the police trace the line?" Kevin asked.

Austin's jaw tightened. The last thing he probably wanted was bad publicity for the show, but calling the police had ended up being a dead-end anyway.

I shook my head, "They said the threat didn't warrant the use of police resources."

"Police resources?" Kevin bit out angrily. "It's a fucking line trace! It would take ten seconds on a TRS-80! When did they call you?"

"This morning. Right after you left."

"What does she mean after you left?" Austin stiffened, his voice anxious and tight.

Kevin looked at him, "I went to see her where she works."

Austin grew irrationally irritated, "What makes you think it's within the scope of your contract to contact Brianna outside of the studio?"

"I don't know, *Austin*," It became obvious real fast that Kevin didn't like to be spoken down to. "Why the fuck would her boss think it was appropriate to send her roses?"

Austin's eyes darted over to mine.

"It was completely on topic," I backpedalled. "We were talking about flowers last night and I might have mentioned that I had just gotten some from you. Off camera, of course. Thank you, by the way. For the roses."

His eyes went back to Kevin, who was staring at him with an accusing eyebrow.

"They were a thank you gift," Austin replied tightly to Kevin.

"*Roses* were a thank you gift?" Kevin snorted a sardonic laugh.

"The fact remains," Austin spoke, emphasizing each word angrily. "That you need to stay away from her outside of this studio. She is competing with two other women to marry you, and if you are seen together…"

"Yeah, yeah," Kevin waved him off. "But let me make one thing clear right now, mister executive producer. As long as this woman is in the running to be my wife, that makes her my fiancée. *My territory.* So back the fuck off with the roses. *Capiche*?"

Austin's face began to turn an angry shade of red—something I had never seen before. But I didn't wait for his reaction.

"Your *territory?*" I exclaim indignantly. I stood up, furiously shaking my head, "I'm sorry, Austin. This man is too ridiculous to continue faking an interest in."

"Faking an interest?" Kevin yelled back at me. "You're doing a shitty job at it!"

Austin stood up and slammed his hands on the top of his desk, his expression unbearably tense.

"Sit down!" He shouted in a voice I had never heard him use before.

Kevin and I exchanged silent glares after we sat.

Austin paced over to the window and stared out over the parking lot below, and I knew he was trying to calm himself down before speaking to us.

With Austin's back turned, I stuck my tongue out at Kevin, but instead of the angry response I expected from him, he grinned back at me and playfully reached out to grab at my tongue with his fingers.

Austin finally turned toward us, his hands grasped behind his back.

"I respectfully request that you refrain from using de-humanizing terms for the women in this contest. Referring to them as your territory is extremely offensive and will not be tolerated." Kevin went to speak but Austin raised his hand to keep him silent. "And, Brianna. The terms of breaking your contract with this company are very clearly spelled out. If you walk out on this show, the resulting lawsuit will financially ruin you."

Kevin slouched sideways in his chair, giving Austin a challenging glare.

"Wonderful." I puffed out a long breath and shook my head. "Can't you fire me or something?"

"No," he replied with his typical pleasant smile.

"Why not?"

He walked over to me and placed his hands on the arms of my chair, leaning toward me, his nose brushing against mine as he murmured, "Because I will not let you go."

He smelled incredible and I could feel myself melting from his proximity to me.

I could also feel the heat of Kevin's glare as he watched us.

Austin stood.

"If you don't want to win this competition, then you will have to do whatever it takes to lose."

Kevin grunted out a laugh and Austin narrowed his eyes on him, "I suggest you think very carefully about who you choose in your next round or you may find yourself in a very uncomfortable position."

"Is that a threat?" Kevin asked.

Austin replied, "No, Mr. Thomas—it's professional advice."

Kevin stood and shoved the chair away, storming out the door and slamming it behind him.

I also stood to leave.

"Brianna," Austin's voice was very quiet.

He looked down at the floor and when he looked up at me again, his eyes were burning with need. I was paralyzed by his stare as he slowly backed me toward the wall.

He moved his full and pouty lips nearer to mine, his swoon-worthy smell encompassing me.

My heart began to pound faster and faster as he slid his

hand to the back of my neck.

"I know this is wrong, but please…" he whispered against my lips. "…don't make me suffer any longer." His seductive words fell from his mouth like poetry, and I wondered how often he had recited these same words to other women in my position.

When he pressed his lips hard against mine, I opened up for him and he began to kiss me more slowly and deeply than my racing heart could stand. He groaned against my mouth, pulling my leg up around his waist and slowly rocking against my heated body where it met his. His lust for me was palpable and even though I was sure I was only one of many women he had seduced this way, he made me believe I was the center of his universe.

"So fucking beautiful," he breathed out desperately.

The buzzer on his desk rang out and I pulled away slightly, leaving him to trail his kisses down my neck until I opened my eyes and saw Kevin propped in the doorway with folded arms, watching us with a lifted eyebrow.

Austin nonchalantly backed away from me, letting my leg slide back down. He adjusted his tie and slowly walked back to his desk before he pushed the button on his intercom. "Yes, Regina?"

"I just wanted to let you know…Mr. Thomas is on his way back up to your office."

He glanced over at Kevin then at me, a smirk touching the corner of his mouth.

"Yes, I see that. Thank you."

Trax

The fucker had the audacity to quirk a smile.

"Did you forget something, Mr. Thomas?"

I looked over at Brianna who was now sitting on the couch looking like she had been caught red-handed smoking a cigarette, but was still trying to wave away the smoke to hide it.

"What kind of game are you playing here?" I asked, trying to keep my temper under control.

This guy was making out with the woman his company promised me.

A woman I can't seem to stop thinking about, and seeing her pinned up against that wall, her face flushed pink and her lips swollen with need? Shit, I'd never be able to *not* see that —it was hot as fuck. Only the next time I saw her that way, I wanted the front row experience because if I saw it any other way again I might just lose my shit.

"What happens in my office is none of your business," Austin said, reminding me how badly I wanted to beat the hell out of him on a normal day; but today I *really* wanted to fuck him up.

"Like hell it ain't." I stepped further into the office. "I'm marrying this girl in four weeks and I find you in here shoving your tongue down her throat?"

Brianna stood up, her eyes flicking between the two of us. "You can't just decide to marry me, Kevin. We haven't even gone through the other rounds!"

"Newsflash, doll face. It's happening."

"Have you talked this decision over with your PR manager?" Austin asked, leaning back and twisting his chair slowly from side to side.

"Why the hell should I? He ain't the one marrying her."

"Mmm," Austin said, clearly not interested in anything except watching the girl—my girl—walking across the room toward the door.

She slammed it closed behind her and I turned back to Austin.

"What the hell kind of man pimps out the girl he's trying to fuck?" I keep my voice low, just in case she can still hear me.

"The kind whose hands are tied." He stood up and crossed the room toward me, finally showing a little fire. "Do you think I wanted to fuck everything up?"

"No, I think you wanted to fuck *her*. Maybe you already have—I really don't give a shit. All I know is whatever's going on between you ends the minute I marry her."

He scoffed and walked back toward the window, propping against it with one arm.

"If you break my contract and this wedding doesn't happen, I'll take you and this company for every goddamn cent you have!"

"We're done here, Mr. Thomas. Please see yourself out."

Austin

He slammed the door when he left.

Nothing is more irritating than a person who slams the door on another man's ever-wavering sense of right and wrong.

The snake inside me is coiling and Kevin Thomas is standing dangerously close to a strike.

I am trying my best to be patient, but I can still taste her on my lips and feel her against my groin and now my craving for her has deepened in a way I can no longer ignore.

I understand his anger. His posessiveness.

Of all the men in the world, I'm the only one who understands how her sweet addiction can creep into your soul until you're lying in your bed, groaning for her under a blanket of hot, sticky need; agonizing for a fix to take away the pain.

I stand by the window, staring down at the parking lot.

I begin to crack my knuckles one at a time, working the pain across my hand as I count the wrongs that are piling up against me.

Pop! I had been given repeated assurance that Kevin Thomas was not interested in leaving this show with a wife.

Snap! I had been provided with a description of a very specific type of woman that should have guaranteed his lack of interest in the third girl—*Snap!*—my girl—*Pop!* who only belongs to me.

I will not let another man have her. Not Kevin Thomas. *Pop!* Not fucking Neil Malone. *Snap!* And not that fucker who took her on a date a few years ago. *Snap!*

He and I had a little chat that night.

Snap!

Very much like the chat Neil and I had the night I caught him coming out of her apartment.

Pop! Snap!

He and I now have an understanding about what is mine and what is not his.

But my confidence in this understanding with Neil is beginning to waver, and I'm starting to wonder if I need to reiterate our last conversation in a more memorable way.

It was Neil who had suggested contacting Freddy about signing Kevin Thomas for the show.

"Your ratings will skyrocket," he had said. And I, in my fucking ignorance, had listened to him.

I did not foresee having to replace one of the contestants at the last minute with the only woman on earth I could not spare to lose to this man.

In my desperation I kissed her. Tasted her. Felt her warm body beneath my hands even though I had promised myself I would wait. I would wait. *I would fucking wait.*

I shutter as I recall her heated eyes, begging me to take what is already mine.

Begging me to unleash a monster that I can not unleash.

I cannot go back to being someone she walks past on the street but does not see.

A stranger who watches her window at night until the flickering blue light against her blinds goes dark. Who slides his fingers around the handle of her door knowing that it was her hands that had last touched the same cool metal. Who presses his ear against her locked door, knowing that somewhere on the other side, she is breathing quiet breaths and sleeping in the soft, warm bed he fantasizes about fucking her in if she would only unlock the door for him one time…*just…one…time.*

I groan, gripping my hair with both hands and pull until the pain makes me cry out.

I brought her too fucking close to me.

The phone on my desk rings and when I look at the caller display I yank it from the receiver and scream into it, "You fucking swore to me that he wasn't going to get married!"

Freddy seems stunned by my words at first.

"He never told me nothing about getting married."

"You tell him that he needs to fucking end this, Freddy!" The pulse in my head begin throbbing. "Or I will end him right the fuck now!"

"Whoa, whoa, calm down! First off, that ain't the way it works with Trax." Freddy replied, like he didn't give a single shit that my patience was crumbling under the intensity of my tremors.

"Fuck how it works with him!" I yell out, picking up a weighted tape dispenser from my desk and throwing it at the door.

"What's the big fucking deal, man?" Freddy asks, "So he gets married? Your ratings will go through the fucking roof!"

I scream at the top of my lungs, my voice cracking, "He's going to marry *Brianna*!"

Freddy was silent on the other end of the line.

I was writhing on the inside, saliva running down my chin as I panted like an animal, trying to calm myself down.

His voice was quiet and hesitant. "Brianna, as in…?"

"As in *my fucking Brianna!*"

"Shit," I heard him bite out in a quiet voice.

"You had better fix this, Freddy!" Hot, angry tears soaked my face as I pounded my fist down on the desk. "You had better fucking fix this or I will put you in the fucking ground with him, do you fucking hear me?"

"Alright, look," he began backpedaling. "The guy's a selfish fuck. The kind of guy who wants to play with other people's toys just because he can. If he thinks you're into her, you're screwed. If you lose interest in her, he'll lose interest in her. You hear me?"

"He's going to fucking marry her." My voice was more controlled now, but my anger hadn't subsided at all and my tears were almost choking me.

"No, he ain't," He said with a certainty even he didn't believe. "I'm telling you, this marriage won't happen. He'll bail at the last minute. Just do what I'm telling you to do and he'll drop her faster than his fans would drop him if he got married."

I slammed the phone down onto the receiver.

Neil

"We got ourselves a problem."Freddy yelled as he flew into my office looking like he had run the entire distance from his office across town. He was profusely sweating and his tie hung loose around his neck, so I was under no illusion that he was exaggerating.

I pushed the button under my desk and the door to my office closed behind him.

"Talk to me," I said, waving toward the chair in front of my desk.

He sat and leaned forward, covering his eyes with his hand, still trying to catch his breath. Every second that his behavior went unexplained felt more and more like my own noose was being hung somewhere.

"You look like shit, man, what's going on?" I pushed.

"It's the little psycho," he finally said, choking up—his eyes glistening with fear.

My smartwatch suddenly alerted me to a spike in my heart rate.

"Austin?" I whispered, as if saying his name too loudly would summon him straight to my door.

The little psycho was the name Freddy and I had used for

Austin ever since his confrontation with me outside of Brie's apartment four years earlier. I had just left after an hour of arguing about a divorce I refused to give her, when he literally appeared out of nowhere like a goddamn stalker.

He had only ever seen her one time for less than a minute at the video lab the night he had come to pick me up then he had been asking all kinds of questions about her. I figured he wanted to hook up with her, but as far as I knew, he hadn't.

"Did you fuck her?"

His eyes seemed off and I remember thinking how strange his voice sounded, like he was joking with me but also dead serious. Being the asshole that I am, I tried to make more out of it than it had actually been. "You never know."

The minute I answered him, shit got real.

He grabbed me and slammed me against the wall, asking me again if I fucked her.

His eyes were fucking crazy.

He didn't even wait for an answer before he jammed something sharp into my thigh. I screamed out in pain and started to freak the fuck out when the son of a bitch gripped my fucking throat in his claws. I felt my own blood running down into my shoe and I swore to him that I had zero interest in fucking Brie; that she was too young, she was a student, that I was actually fucking *gay*—hell, you name it and I staked my innocence on it.

After lying my ass off about why I was there he eventually let me go. But *fuck*! I didn't need to be told twice—from then on, I kept the fuck away from her. It made it a hell of a lot more difficult to try and convince her why she shouldn't divorce me, but what the fuck ever.

It ain't like I was being all sentimental and trying to keep the woman I love from walking out on me. Shit, no. It was more like I was trying to keep my ass on the money train and maybe fuck her just for the hell of it—until the little psycho fucked up that part of the plan, but that's whatever.

People had been throwing money and awards at Brianna ever since she made that video and I wanted in on a piece of the fucking pie, so I manipulated her into marrying me in Vegas then signed my name to a lucrative deal, *on behalf of my beloved wife*, that she knew nothing about.

After it became clear that Austin was obsessed with the chick, I thought it best to keep my mouth zipped shut about Vegas. I warned Freddy not to say a damn word to anyone about it and knew there was no way in hell Brie would be saying anything to anyone—she was too fucking ashamed of herself for falling for my shit.

Every few months or so she'll send me divorce papers and I'll send them back to her unsigned; but that's the most I've heard from her.

A divorce would shine a spotlight on my studio. The one *her* money paid for with the money she never knew existed, thanks to Freddy and the shady-ass accountants who work with him.

There was no divorce in our future—none that I would willingly submit to.

Austin hadn't said one word to me about Brie ever since that night. He never said one word about my bitched up leg—never even acted like he remembered threatening me. But that don't mean the fucker ever let go of that shit. Neither have I, but I'm too scared of his crazy ass to say shit to him, so I just make nice and keep as far away from the fucker as I possibly can.

Now with Freddy coming in here looking like death is hovering over him in a custom fitted suit, he's got me feeling a little more than on edge.

"This is all your fucking fault," Freddy yells, jamming a finger in my direction before he gets up and begins pacing around the room.

Shit, he's scared.

No—he's fucking *terrified*!

Shit.

"You put him straight on me, you piece of shit!"

"What are you talking about?" I demand, leaning my forearms on my desk. "You're getting a bigger cut than Trax on this deal! That's how this works—you help me, I help you, and we both get rich."

He stopped pacing and gripped the back of the chair he had been sitting in, piercing me with his terrified expression, "Yeah, until for some goddamned fucking reason, Trax has decided to go through with the fucking wedding!"

"So he marries some broad on TV? Who the hell cares?"

His eyes pin me to my chair, and his words freeze me to the core.

"The woman he's marrying is *Brianna*."

Silence hung in the air like a circling vulture and I felt myself swallow hard.

"Brianna?" Her name barely audible as my hands began to tremble as uncontrollably as my voice. "Brie? Brianna? *My wife*, Brianna?"

"The very same."

He shoved the chair with a jerk then began pacing again until my nerves could no longer take it. He turned to me, "Neil, he's going to put you in a fucking box."

I nodded my head only once, slightly.

"You need to get the hell out of this town as fast as your car will take you. Change your name. Leave the fucking country. Shit, I don't know. But what I do know is that he's going to fucking kill you if he finds you."

I pulled at my collar uneasily, letting the warmth that had been building up under my shirt steam out from beneath my chin.

I shook my head in refusal.

"No," I said, "No. This is *my* studio, *my* money, *my* wife!"

"Your wife?" Freddy scoffed. "When's the last time you even talked to her? Is she really worth dying for?"

"I could give a shit about her." I said, walking to the window. I waved my hand toward the parking lot. "I built this. I made this happen. *Me*. And I'm not giving it up. Not to him, not to her."

"Her money built this." Freddy points out.

"Her and her husband's money," I corrected.

"If they look hard enough they'll see that the date of your wedding falls several days after the date of that paperwork. That makes it her money."

"If they look hard enough. But they won't have any reason to look if I don't give her a divorce. She doesn't even know that money existed."

"Fine. Supposing all that slips under the radar. You're forgetting the most important thing; you tricked the little psycho's obsession into marrying you and then you hid it from him for four years."

I shoved my hands in my pockets and stared at the wall for a long time.

"Like you said; it's been four years. Knowing Austin, he's probably moved on to someone else."

"He hasn't," Freddy said. "And when he finds out that Trax ain't his real competition?" He pulled his finger beneath his neck.

"He's crazy, but he's not stupid." I turned to face Freddy. "He's not going to kill me. He may beat my ass, sure, but he won't kill me."

"Whatever you say, man." Freddy laughed, shaking his head like I was blind. He opened the door and turned to me. "It's your funeral."

The sound of the door clicking closed behind him sent a shiver up my spine.

Brianna

The tension between Kevin and Austin was being felt in every department.

While Austin stood off-set glaring at Kevin, Kevin didn't help matters by sitting on-set acting like the whole world, beginning with Austin, could go fuck itself.

It was the day of the visual competition and I was still holding out hope that maybe he had come to his senses.

The two other girls were both gorgeous women.

If Kevin was going to make the most of this opportunity, his best bet would be to pick each woman at least one time like his fans expected, blow off the wedding, and remain a bachelor.

Nobody wanted to see him settling down with *Plain Jane* in Suburbia—least of all, Jane herself.

Tiffinni and Brandi had been hand selected for him, but whatever that sheet had said, these women weren't his type at all. It only took one night of talking to him without cameras around for me to see that clear as day. But that didn't mean I was his type, either.

I was option C—the lesser of three huge mistakes.

I just didn't understand why he felt he had to choose any

of us.

I pulled out my phone when I heard an incoming text.

TRAX: I'm so fucking jealous of him

BRIE: It was a mistake

TRAX: I want to kiss you like that

BRIE: Then don't pick me. Fair trade?

TRAX: #LongTermGoals

BRIE: You know there's a great big world of women out there

TRAX: There's only one Brie

I rolled my eyes.

What Kevin was enamored with was the instantaneous connection we shared.

I felt it too. It felt like the beginning of something; not quite love, not quite friendship, but something that will change you.

He probably didn't get too many opportunities in his line of work to explore these kinds of connections. If I were to guess, they all ended up as one night stands, which didn't help him learn to differentiate which feelings were surface and which ones could have been deeper if left to grow.

To him, every positive connection with a female ended in sex, and sex ended every positive connection.

I was likely the first woman who didn't reward him with the result he expected and because of that his eyes were now focused on me as he worked through understanding these new feelings.

It obviously didn't help that he walked in on Austin kissing me. When I hadn't let Kevin kiss me, he had probably convinced himself it was just the way I was. But then he saw Austin and I, and suddenly realized that he was being denied what other men were not.

Now the two men are in a tug-of-war over a prize that neither of them really want; they just want the glory of taking it away from the other.

My internship had officially ended three days earlier, and Austin had signed off on the paperwork. I received an email earlier that day confirming that I had officially completed all of my degree requirements and in two weeks, I could pick up my diploma at the school.

As soon as this show wrapped up, I would cash my check and start packing my bags for Anywhere, USA. I had already put in the request to terminate my lease just to make sure I didn't do something stupid like change my mind and stay.

I was so over California.

While I loved the diversity of Hollywood, the films they made here weren't the kinds of films I wanted to be making. New York would hold more possibilities, but the idea of moving to another fast-paced, high-cost-of-living city turned me off.

More than anything, I just wanted to settle in a place where if I smiled at somebody, they'd smile back and it would be genuine.

Smiles weren't free in Hollywood and more often than not they were made of gilded rot. Everyone in the industry either had a knife in their hand or one in their back, except for those rare and special few who were able to rise above the bullshit or were smart enough to leave.

There was only one giant complication I had to deal with before I could pick up and move on with my life, and if I could somehow talk Kevin out of this whole marriage thing, it would make that task a lot less pressing.

Tiffinni's formalwear disaster had set the tone for the rest of the evening.

The harsh studio lighting bounced off every silver sequin on her dress, reflecting thousands of shimmering polka dots on her face and everywhere else.

Under ordinary circumstances it wouldn't have been so funny, but she took herself so seriously in her attempt to look sexy, that it was the comedic equivalent to Marilyn Monroe singing to the president with a giant booger in her nose.

Austin growled at the lighting guys, knowing it had been completely intentional. The sound and light crews were all team Brianna, but as flattering as that was, sabotaging the other women wasn't going to help me in the least.

Luckily, Brandi's dress was much less flamboyant and was actually quite pretty for something with a mid-80's flare.

My dress was going to take home the formalwear bronze medal and if I was lucky maybe I would get a hearty boo from the audience.

There was no way I was going to win this round—no way on earth he would be justified in picking me. I was forcing his hand, and Fabiano was already cracking open the smelling salts, preparing himself for the outfit he had been so adamantly opposed to my wearing.

I walked confidently onto the set in a plain patterned mennonite-style frock, wearing thick beige stockings and plain loafers. My hair was parted down the middle and clipped back in two tiny barettes, and I had refused Wanda's freckle-concealing make-up—high-def viewers be damned.

Unfortunately, my choice of formal wear had the exact opposite effect on Kevin than I had expected, and I realized very quickly that it was my snarky sense of humor he was attracted to.

What that meant was that I was funnier to him than Tiffinni and Brandi were gorgeous, which put me at yet another disadvantage because I did not know how to turn off snarky-me.

Humor was my primary defense mechanism when I was uncomfortable and since the moment this show began I have been nothing *but* uncomfortable.

At the side of the set, Austin wore a disapproving frown on his face.

I was making a complete mockery of the show he had worked extremely hard to put together. A show that was supposed to be lighthearted, like *The Dating Game*. Unfortunately, it was now a show about Brianna making an ass out of herself to deter the attention of a man who is determined to choose her anyway.

All I could hope for was that Austin would get so angry with me that he would fire me from the show and replace me with a woman who was actually able to follow through on the obligations of her binding contract.

This would end his interest in me, and it would also end the tug-of-war.

I would be packing my stuff in boxes and rolling out by the end of the week.

I had just finished flat-ironing my hair, when my dressing room was pushed open by Austin who entered then slammed the door closed behind him.

I grabbed for a robe to cover my bra and panties, but he yanked it out of my hand and threw it over the back of a chair.

"I want to see what you're wearing for the next round. *Now.*"

His voice was uncharacteristically angry.

"Fabiano hasn't brought it over yet," I replied nervously, feeling the weight of his stare.

"If you think wearing this kind of shit is going to change his mind, you're sorely mistaken." He grabbed the ugly frock and dropped it on the floor like it disgusted him. "If you have to marry him, then get a fucking annulment." My guts churned at those words. "But quit pretending he won't see how beautiful you are under all of that shit, *because he fucking does*. Every person on this goddamned earth sees your beauty and it's *my fault*." He slammed his fist into his chest angrily.

The tears that came into my eyes burned hot at his scolding, making me feel so incredibly ashamed of myself. I covered my face with my hands, "I just feel so trapped, and I'm doing everything I can to escape."

He pulled my hands away from my face, his breath hitching as his eyes met mine. He pressed his lips to each of my tear-covered cheeks.

This was so wrong.

So, so wrong.

There was another knock at the door and he stepped away from me, walking several paces across the room. I picked up my robe and covered myself, quickly wiping the rest of my tears away.

"Come in," I said.

Fabiano entered the room with my next outfit over his arm and a frown on his face, noticing my tears.

"Baby girl, I'd be crying too if I had to wear this."

"I won't be wearing that," I gestured to the outfit on his arm, unable to meet his eyes.

He sighed in relief, placing a hand upon his chest, "Oh sweet heavens, hallelujah. She came to her senses."

"Can you pick something out for me?" I asked.

"I'll do it." Austin growled, pushing past Fabiano.

Fabiano turned his eyes back on me and tsk'd at me, "You poked the bear, didn't you?"

I nodded.

"Mmm…Maybe you'll get lucky and the bear will poke back."

The bear poked back in the form of a low-cut, figure hugging, floor length red satin dress with slits cut to the top of my thighs. It's the kind of dress that would be gorgeous on a curvy model, but on me it felt nearly as ridiculous as the original outfit I had picked out.

"What the hell am I wearing?" I asked, while Wanda did her magic on me, applying fake eyelashes and winged eyeliner to my eyes as well as a few glued-on gems, making me look like a 50's Hollywood diva.

"Mm-mm, is all I'm saying," she said, squeezing her lips together and shaking her head. "You're a knockout."

"Austin is punishing me for the Amish getup."

"More like he's punishing himself," She sprayed my hair. "Alright, go get 'em, hot stuff."

I stood up and wobbled, forgetting I was wearing heels.

F-ing heels!

As I walked up to the edge of the set waiting for my cue to come on-camera, I heard the entire studio go quiet except for the sound of someone dropping a pen.

I glanced toward Austin, then toward Kevin, both wearing similar wide-eyed expressions on their faces.

The sound of Heath clearing his throat broke through the virtual sound of chirping crickets. The show's announcer looked around the room, wondering if he should begin or not.

"Fuck this," Kevin stood up and paced off the set angrily, throwing his hand in the air toward me, "She wins."

Heath asks, "What the hell's going on?"

Kevin stands with his fist planted on his hip and runs his other hand over his mouth before he points at me from across the room, "You see the way that woman's dressed?"

I looked down at my dress.

Heath looked over at me in confusion, "Yeah?"

Kevin growls, "Put some fucking clothes on her!"

While the dress was revealing, it wasn't as if I was standing there naked. Did he have a problem with me looking...*sexy*?

Heath looked at the production staff and lifted his arms out like he was entirely confused by what was going on.

Austin stepped forward, a slight smirk on his face, "What's the matter with the way she's dressed? You didn't seem to complain when she was dressed like an Amish girl."

Kevin glared at Austin, "I don't want her dressed like that on TV."

"I've seen photos of you with women who were wearing a lot less than that," Austin provoked, in an attempt to remind everyone—more specifically me—that Kevin wasn't the upstanding man he was trying to be at that moment.

"She's not a fucking groupie, Austin," Kevin hissed under his breath.

Austin got in Kevin's face and stared him straight in the eye, *"Exactly."*

Very carefully I made my way over in my painfully elegant red spiked heels.

"She's suffering in those," Kevin reached down and grabbed my foot, nearly throwing me off balance as he pulled my shoe off and tossed it across the set. He reached for my other foot and rather than let him take it off for me, I slipped it off myself and let it drop to the floor beside me.

He looked over at Heath then back at Austin.

"She's beautiful! Look at her," he waved his hand over my dress, "*She's a fucking goddess*. But she is *not* like those other two. She's trying to become a respectable film-maker. When all this is over, I don't think this outfit is going to help her career at all. Some seedy producer is going to hire her based on this outfit alone...*and then what?*"

Austin just stared back at him, chewing on the inside of his mouth.

Kevin looked up at me, "Darling, do you feel comfortable wearing that?"

I shrugged, "No, not necessarily."

He looked back up at them, "You see? Let her change. Go put something else on, Brie."

"Go change." Austin jerked his head toward the dressing room, still squinting at Kevin.

I closed the door of my dressing room as I waited for Fabiano.

I looked down at my phone.

TRAX: Fuck, Brie, Fuck

BRIE: Thank you

TRAX: You fucking ruined me for other women

BRIE: Sorry?

Trax

What the hell was Austin trying to pull, dressing Brie up like Jessica Rabbit?

If he was trying to dissuade me from choosing her, he took the wrong damn avenue.

The girl was a wet fucking dream, and fuck yes I'll be picturing her like that again later, but right now it was supposed to look like I was giving my full attention to all three of them.

All through the damn filming, Tiffinni and Brandi were flaunting their surgically enhanced racks at me, and yeah they're both gorgeous women, but my mind kept going back to that red dress and *fuck me,* all those freckles.

Whoever the hell thought it was a good idea to cover that shit up with makeup was not going to find themselves on my Christmas card list this year.

I was sitting there with my elbows on my knees staring at the floor while waiting through another painfully boring round of clothing changes when I hear that Tilly chick talking with Heath about stirring up shit in wardrobe so that the other two dimwits look more like my Brie.

My Brie.

When the hell did that happen in my mind?

One completely innocent night in the hot tub, admiring her sweet ass in a bikini, and now my subconscious is invested in this woman, too?

I let my mind begin to wander, thinking about what kind of date I was planning to take her on this week.

Yes, I will be picking her again, no matter what they do to disguise them other chicks.

They aren't the kind of women that catch my interest.

The kind of woman I'm drawn to isn't one you could pick out of a crowd on first sight. To other people, Brie's a daisy in a field of daisies. But once she gets inside your head, she shines like the brightest star in the sky and you can't fucking turn your eyes away—you can't *not* see her.

I don't have a hell of a lot of opportunities to get to know women that come and go in my life. It's even harder for me to start up a conversation because of my personality type, so what that leaves me with is the luck of time and place.

I'd have never called being on this show *luck*, but hell, maybe I can call it fate.

Maybe having this chance to get to know a woman I feel a crazy strong attraction to is what's been written in the cards for me.

Brianna

"And so we meet again," I smile, but I know it doesn't reach my eyes.

With a low whistle, Kevin's appreciative gaze travels over my body and the shimmering dress Fabiano had picked out for me to wear. "Damn! Look at you."

I look down at myself, half-smiling, "I know. It's a bit much."

"You're totally rocking the dress," he said, taking my hand. "But I got a feeling it's not what you would have picked out."

I blew a stray hair out of my face and looked off the the side.

He ran a callused finger down the tip of my nose, "Did I piss you off saying that?"

I shook my head.

"No, you're right. If it were up to me, I would have worn those fuzzy comfortable pajamas I wore on the show last week."

He bit his lower lip, "I've thought a lot about your ass in those pajamas."

I narrowed my eyes, "Are you making a pass at me, Mr. Thomas?"

"I am if you're letting me."

"I'm not."

One of the cameramen began laughing so hard at my rejection of him that he had to lower his camera and let the other one take over.

It felt like we were flirting—why was I flirting with this man?

"So where are you taking me tonight?" I asked as we began walking side by side, trying to ignore the fact that there were cameras and mics all around us.

"I thought we'd hit the Santa Monica pier. Maybe go for a walk."

"Wow," I said, glancing toward him. "I won't be getting shot at with paintballs tonight?"

He chuckled, "Admit it, nobody has ever taken you on that kind of date before."

I felt my cheeks turn pink.

Nobody had taken me on any kind of date—*ever*.

My parents had been too strict to let me date in high school and I had been so focused on trying to help Mika in my first year of college that I didn't have time for dating. Then Neil came along with his handsome face and said a few flattering words to me and the next thing I know I've been sweet-talked into marrying him.

After the one date I had since Neil ghosted me, I had completely written off guys altogether.

Not that I wasn't attracted to them, I just accepted that they were more trouble than they were worth. This whole thing with Kevin nearly blindsided me, and needless to say I was having a hard time believing his sincere interest.

"You're right." I finally said. "I'm pretty sure I still have some bruises."

"That's why we did the hot tub afterwards." He slid his arm around my waist as we walked toward the limo, leaning closer to my ear so the camera didn't pick up his words, "The only bruise I still have is the one on my ego."

I glanced at him as he opened the limo door for me. I slid in and he followed, handing me a shoe box.

"What's this?" I ask, opening the lid on a new pair of Chuck Taylors. "You're giving me shoes?"

"Isn't that a normal second-date gift?"

I was genuinely smiling, little laughs escaping me even as I tried to hold them back.

I tilted my head at him, "From you, they are absolutely normal. But please don't tell me you're taking me to play basketball."

His unexpected charm kept me on my toes, and in some ways it felt like I had met my match. He wasn't boring and predictable—and I *liked* that.

His eyes sparkled back at me.

"Hey, don't tell Tiffinni I bought you sneakers for our beach date, alright?"

I snorted, leaning forward to take off my flats. He reached down and pulled my bare feet into his lap, putting the Chucks on me. It was only then that I realized they had film reels all over them.

I felt genuinely touched by the thoughtfulness that had gone into getting me a gift that was so personal and something in my heart fluttered.

"Thank you," I said quietly. "I really like them."

He shrugged, "Well, I really like you."

Aaaaand…pause frame. Rewind.

What?

I really like you?

The warm and fuzzy feeling that had been building in my chest dissolved abruptly, leaving me feeling slightly disgusted with myself as I realized that all of this was for the benefit of the viewers.

I really like you.

Second to the 'test drive' comment from the hot tub, it was the cheesiest line that had ever existed, and he just dropped it on my head like bird shit after a fly over.

This was not a real date, and I just got a very real reminder that I had to stop thinking of it as one.

I couldn't trust a thing this man said or did because it was all just for show. For bullshit publicity.

I was an idiot to be falling for him and social media was about to slay me wide open.

Brie; the idiot who fell for the rock star only to be dumped for a set of hooters on episode three.

That was what I wanted, wasn't it? For him to stop choosing me?

Hell, I no longer knew what I wanted.

But it didn't matter, because I'd never have it anyway.

I blocked his number the minute I got home.

Trax

"Cut to commercial!" Heath calls out, tossing his clipboard over his shoulder in frustration, nearly hitting one of the boom operators. "Brandi, what the hell are you doing?"

"I'm giving him a massage."

The confused expression in her big, wide-spread eyes as she knelt before me with her hands gripping my inner thighs made me want to pat her head like a puppy.

"This is national television, not the White Leopard Lounge! There are very clear limits as to what can be done on a PG-13 show and you were about six inches away from crossing that line."

"Only two inches away," I said, winking at her and making her giggle.

Heath looked at the otherwise impassive look on my face and I sighed out, rolling my eyes.

After Tiffinni's virtual lap dance a few minutes earlier, it became clear that these two women couldn't seem to figure out that sex isn't going to coerce me into choosing them. Neither is boxed macaroni and cheese, or peanut butter and jelly fucking sandwiches.

Home cooked meals, my ass.

Even Brie failed me on that part of the show, handing me a frozen TV dinner with hand-written instructions on how to cook it in a microwave.

The audience ate that shit up.

I didn't—*because it was fucking frozen*.

Fucking Brie.

"As per the contest rules, I have provided you with a home cooked meal," she said, in that snarky way that makes me want to grab her by the hair and shove my tongue down her throat. "Just pop it in the microwave when you get home and it will cook." Hand propped on her hip, she handed me a note. "Here—I've even written the instructions on a honey-do list."

The note said, *This isn't 1950. Make your own dinner.* It was surrounded with little hearts.

I looked up at her and whispered, "Why'd you block my number, Brie?"

The defiant little lift of her eyebrow only made me want to domesticate the little alley cat even more.

"Fine, then we'll play it that way," I sighed out, taking the frozen meal and tossing it onto the table. "Where's my drink, woman?" I leaned back in my chair and folded my arms over my chest as I peered up at her.

With a hint of fire in her eyes, she walked over to the loaded bar and began making some kind of mixed drink—shaking it, like a professional bartender.

If she was faking what she was doing, she was faking it well.

She gracefully crossed the set and slammed the glass down on the table in front of me. She was pissed at me, that much was for damn sure—only I had no idea what I had done wrong.

I looked down at the glass then back up at her before I took a sip.

"That ain't half bad," I said. "What's it called?"

"An *Angry Wet Rock Star.*"

She made a grab for the glass, but I moved even faster, snatching it up before she could get it. I held the drink away from her. Liquid sloshed out of the glass and began running down my arm while I wrestled my other arm around her waist, both of us laughing as she wriggled to get free.

I poured the drink on her head, knowing damn well it was exactly what she would have done if she had gotten hold of that glass first.

Ice cubes clattered to the floor as she let out a shriek and shoved at my chest. Both of us tumbled onto the fake kitchen floor, landing in the mess—her on top of me, both of us smelling like a distillery.

I let go of her and the glass rolled across the floor. My back ached like a son of a bitch as I slowly eased myself into a sitting position. Every one of my muscles were sore, my stomach cramping from laughing so damn hard. She sat up, flicking the alcohol from her wet fingertips as she gave me that smile—*that fucking smile.*

The chemistry between us was so palpable the whole goddamned country could feel it—*so why couldn't she?*

The host broke into his pre-commercial speil and when we went off the air, I began to laugh like a motherfucker, pointing at her, "You get what you fucking deserve!"

She crawled toward me and shoved my shoulder. I pulled her against me, murmuring in her ear, "I could really use that massage right now—*White Leopard* style. What do you say?" I licked the sticky sweet liquid from her cheek and she jerked away from me, slumping her shoulders and giving into more laughter despite her attempt at holding it in.

Joelle came onto the set, "Brie, you have three minutes to go change your shirt and rinse out your hair. You..." she waved her hand toward the bulge in my jeans. "...take care of *that.*"

Brie hurried to her dressing room and I caught sight of Austin, slouched in a director's chair with his chin propped in his hand, doing nothing to hide his searing glare at me.

Brie came back to the set wearing tight jeans and a fitted black v-neck with the Chevron Dreams logo on it. I knew it was rooted in sarcasm, but seeing her in my band's shirt was seriously fucking hot.

"Lie down," she commanded in a sharp voice and every part of me responded in obedience, lying face down on a massage table they'd brought in, knowing there was no way in hell they could pull off a PG-13 chair massage when this girl finally decided to put her hands on me.

I felt a cold, hard object gliding up my spine then a sudden rush of cold air hit my back. She had cut my shirt open with a pair of scissors…*oh, this is so fucking happening between us.*

She began rubbing at the tight muscles on my back and shoulders with some warm goo and my entire body went limp, melting beneath her hands.

I turn my head to the side and gazed up at her freckled face.

So fucking beautiful. So. Fucking. Beautiful.

I reached down and began massaging the inside of her thigh, not giving a shit that the cameras were still rolling on us. As I lay there I realized how much I honestly wanted this woman. Just being able to touch her without her pulling away sent little waves of electricity shooting to every limb. I wanted a future with her. I wanted something real. And she wasn't going to give in without a shove.

I felt myself sigh out the words, "Will you marry me?"

Her hands slowed and she looked down at my face, terror etched in her expression, "What?"

I pull my hand away from her and sat up.

I couldn't look at her because I knew she was going to be

furious with me.

"I'm sorry, babe…I have to…"

I look toward the camera and say to the host, "I'm choosing Brie for the third time. She's mine."

Brianna

She's mine.

The words seemed foreign, and I barely heard them when Kevin pulled the cut fabric away from the front of his chest, showing off his chiseled abs.

I could literally hear the sound of ratings skyrocketing, of women swooning, of his fans scowling—of Tiffinni and Brandi's hopes hitting the floor. I knew somewhere out there, Gabby was in need of resuscitation.

We were now five weeks into the show and I was no closer to getting Neil to sign the divorce papers than I had been four years ago. Even *with* his signature, a divorce would take a minimum of six months for the courts to finalize.

Kevin was staring at me like he had betrayed me, but how could I be mad at him when I knew there was so much more that he was doing this for. The amount of money that was said to be on the line for The Marietta Center was approaching nearly 14 million dollars.

If Neil hadn't been an issue, those donations alone would have been enough to convince me to go along with it. Hell, I had married someone I didn't even like for a lot less.

But I couldn't play along—it was literally impossible.

I had to find another way around the terms of my contract. I had to convince Austin to fake the legitimacy of the wedding—even if it had to be temporary.

I balled Kevin's torn shirt in my hand and stood behind him, wiping the massage gel off of his muscular back.

I rested my chin on his shoulder as people milled around us on the set.

He turned his head toward me and smiled an easy, apologetic smile.

"What do you want to do on our third date?" I asked, casually.

"Fuck like rabbits," he deadpanned, sending my pulse racing off the charts.

Trax

"What's on your mind, Miss Rose?"

She wore her feelings in the eyes she wouldn't show me. She only gave me a slight shake of her head.

I had texted her fifty fucking times since the third round ended, telling her I was sorry, but she hadn't replied to a single one. Hell, I guess I was lucky enough that she unblocked me, but I wanted to know that she didn't hate me.

"Look," I sighed out, scratching at my short beard. "I know you're pissed. But every thing about this tells me it's right."

She finally lifted her eyes to me, "Kevin, we barely know each other."

"I barely know a lot of people and I make multi-million dollar deals with them all the time."

"This isn't a multi-million dollar deal," she replied, folding a cloth napkin and calmly placing it on her lap.

"Why don't you want to take a chance on me?" I saw the camera crew getting ready to begin filming, and threw my arm over the back of the booth.

"It's not you, Kevin," she said quietly.

"Never heard that one before." I chuckled. "It's pretty much always me."

"I'm just not..." she paused, thinking of the words she wanted to say, "...emotionally available."

I felt my heart drop inside of my chest and swallowed hard, "Are you in love with Austin?"

She seemed surprised by my question and shook her head, "No! And that's not what I mean. I'm not in love with anyone, it's just...I can't do the marriage thing."

I stared at her without saying a word.

This girl's issues were with marriage itself. It's just my fucking luck to finally meet a girl I can't live without only to find out she's the only woman who ever existed that hates marriage.

I knew I was moving too fast for her. But I knew she was the one. Before I even knew what she looked like. It wasn't anything she said, it was just...*I knew.*

And I wasn't even looking for her.

My heart ached when she quirked a sad smile at me.

God, I was such a selfish jackass for doing this to her.

I just wanted more of her sunlight and ended up bringing her clouds.

For the first time, I wanted to peel off a woman's layers more than her clothing.

But the more her layers were shed, the more I found beneath them. She was like a puzzle that became more difficult to solve the closer I got to the answer.

I should have just chosen one of the other girls and taken marriage off the table, but I was afraid if I let her go I'd lose the chance to explore whatever this was between us. The show was forcing us to spend time together that I was pretty damn sure she'd never agree to on her own.

Shit, I honestly didn't even know if she was attracted to me.

She didn't react the way most women do with me; she didn't flirt or touch me or bat her eyes—hell, she didn't even let me kiss her!

It seemed like every goddamned woman on earth wanted a piece of my ass except the girl I actually wanted.

I circled around the table to her side of the booth just before they began filming.

I pushed into the booth next to her and put my arm around her shoulder, leaning in and murmuring in her ear, "Fuck the show, Brie. This is you and me straight talking right now. You say you're emotionally unavailable and that's fine, but I have to know one thing, and I want you to be completely fucking honest with me, alright?"

She nodded and I slipped my hand onto her cheek, pulling her toward me as I leaned in and pressed my lips against the sensitive spot beneath her ear, tasting her sweet skin the way I wanted to taste her lips. I felt her body tremble against mine as she sucked in a deep breath.

I pulled back and saw that her eyes were closed. "Do you feel anything for me at all?"

I circled back to my own seat and she stared across the table at me.

"Yes," she whispered and I let out a breath I had been holding in since I had chosen her for that third time.

The cameras began rolling and our interaction changed instantly to something light and playful and it just felt so fucking fake. I wanted the real Brie—even if she was pissed at me.

The deception ended soon enough and reality came crashing in when she stood to leave.

She ran her hands over her skirt, "I have to go. I have to be at work in a few hours."

"Don't you get tired of waking up so early?" I asked, trying to keep her as long as I could.

She shrugged, "I don't have a choice. Morning is when people want coffee."

"You should be doing the kind of work you're meant to be doing."

A soft laugh came out of her mouth and it broke my heart to hear because it told me she didn't believe in herself—not in the way the girl who made that video had.

Something had stolen her fire and I wanted to be the one to help her find it again.

"Goodnight, Kevin," she said in barely a whisper.

"Brie, wait…" I stood, taking a few steps closer to where she stood and I slid my hands over her shoulders, stopping when they gently grasped her shoulders. I pulled close and pressed my forehead to hers, closing my eyes as I spoke, "I want to be with you. There's something happening between us and whatever it is, it's not something I've ever felt before with anyone else."

I placed my hand on her soft cheek, staring into her glistening eyes, "Give me a chance. Give *us* a chance."

A tear finally fell onto her cheek and without a single word, she turned and walked away from me and I have never felt so goddamned helpless in my life.

Brianna

"Well, well, well...*Mrs. Malone*. How the hell are you?"

I felt my muscles stiffen when his voice came over the line and my temples began to throb with a sharp pain.

"I don't have time for your shit, Neil," I bit out. "I need you to sign those papers. Now. *Today*."

He let out a long sigh, "I'm afraid I can't do that, little wife."

"Why not?" I growled, reliving the same frustrating conversation we'd repeatedly had over the past four years. "Why won't you just give me a divorce? It's not like you have any actual feelings for me."

"Don't be ridiculous, darling. I've always loved you." The amusement in his voice was infuriating. "You haven't called me in months, Brie. Why the sudden urgency? Screwing someone on the side?"

"Fuck you."

He tsk'd me, "Such language. Do I need to come over and wash those dirty words out of that pretty little mouth of yours?"

"Don't be disgusting, Neil," I hissed. "Just give me the divorce."

"How could I possibly let you go when we still have some unfinished business between us? Do you know what I realized? I never even tasted my own wife. You didn't even put out on our wedding night."

"You mean the night you got drunk and tried to force yourself on me? The marriage wasn't real. We made a deal that you would give me an annulment as soon as you got your inheritance. And as a side note; I wouldn't let you touch me if you were the last man on earth."

"As a side note," he mocked me, "You could have said no to marrying me."

"Hindsight is 20/20. I should have seen you for the son of a bitch you are."

"I'm *your* son of a bitch, baby," he chuckled. "Until death do us part."

I always ended up so angry when I talked to him, it was one of the main reasons I had given up trying. The time and effort it took to begin the process of a contested divorce had been too expensive and inconvenient with my already overbooked schedule.

At one point I had just decided that I would wait until I finished school and had more time and money. Never in a million years did I foresee that any of this would happen. And it wasn't like I had a ton of guys knocking down my door for the chance to marry me.

In the four years since Neil tricked me into marrying him I had only had one date. I thought it had gone well, but the guy never called me back and had even blocked my number. I still have no idea why he went to such extreme measures, so I just assumed either he was mad I didn't put out on the first date or that he had been cheating on someone else.

"So Ma's been pushing for grandchildren," Neil said, bringing me back to the conversation. "You game?"

I hung up on him and threw the phone onto the couch in

disgust.

I rubbed my throbbing temples.

I was going to have to tell Austin the truth.

Murray Studios was going to sue me for everything I own—which currently wasn't much more than they had paid me, but the potential to screw me out of all of my future money was there.

Everything I had done was for nothing.

There would be a minimum six month wait to be officially divorced in California, even if he signed the papers right now—which he very clearly wasn't going to do.

I had to break my contract and I laughed out loud because I wanted to cry. I hadn't even wanted to do the show in the first place. I had begged Austin not to make me…and now it was going to cost me everything because I hadn't just put my foot down and told him the truth.

Austin sat with his elbows on his desk, gripping the hair on both sides of his head like he was suffering with a migraine. His eyes were squeezed shut in pain and I felt even worse for what I was about to do, so I lost my nerve and turned around to leave.

"Brianna."

I turned back to find him in the exact same position. How had he known I was there?

He sat back in his chair, his hair a mess, eyes dark underneath and his full lips pink and slightly swollen, like he had been crying.

"Are you alright?" I asked quietly.

He nodded with a smile that came across far too sexy for the mood in the room. He clearly wasn't alright, if anything there was a hunger in his eyes that seemed to be barely contained.

I slowly crossed the room and sat in one of the chairs in

front of his desk.

I felt my body trembling.

I was about to be so financially fucked by this company that I would never be able to recover.

Austin stared at me in silence, watching the range of emotions that must have been crossing my face.

"Austin, I…" I swallowed around the lump in my throat. "I can't get married tomorrow."

He picked up a pen, tapping it on his desk a few times before dropping it and wiping his hand over his mouth and looking toward the window.

"Your contract obligates…" he began, as if reciting a well-rehearsed speech.

"I know what my contract says," I cut him off. "But I'm not saying this because I have cold feet."

"Brianna." He leaned forward. "If you need money for an annulment, I can…"

"No." I shook my head as hot tears blurred my eyes. *Just say it!* "I'm already married."

When I finally found the courage to look at him again, the stillness in his eyes was absolutely terrifying. I had never before seen anger so dark that it manifested itself as the appearance of absolute neutrality.

It made my skin turn to ice.

"Married." He repeated, his voice restrained as the slightest hint of a furious smile twitched at the corners of his trembling lips.

"Yes," I replied, barely able to speak the word.

Everything he had worked for—all the advertising and the planning and the hype—had been building up to this finalé.

The viewer ratings had been record-breaking and it was currently the most-anticipated season finalé on the network. All eyes in Hollywood were watching to see if they would copycat the idea or if it would bust.

My confession must have felt like a hammer, smashing apart his success.

Now, instead of on top of the biggest success of the season, he would be at the bottom of the disaster that was about to unfold.

He swallowed visibly.

His brown eyes glazed over before a single tear fell and hit the desk.

He didn't move his eyes from mine.

His gaze was frightening, but my heart shattered for him.

"Since when?" His whisper was gravelly and so very defeated. My reply didn't come fast enough for him and the sudden increase in the volume and intensity of his voice made my body jolt with surprise. "*Since when*, Brianna?"

"Four years ago," I admitted meekly.

He stood, shaking his head in complete denial of my words as he shoved his chair backward. "Then why haven't I ever seen him?" He yelled. "Why the fuck haven't I ever seen him, Brianna?"

The tone of his question not only scared, but confused me.

He came around the desk and stood in front of me, gripping the arms of my chair and trapping me. He moved his face close to mine as he scowled at me, accentuating every word, "Who. Is. He?"

My voice wavered, "Someone I knew from school. The marriage was supposed to be annulled, but he never went through with it. He refuses to give me a divorce."

A terrifying look of realization flashed across his eyes and he jerked to a stand, turning away from me.

"Fuuuuck!" He screamed like he was crazed, putting an angry fist through the drywall in his office. His nose was now bleeding from the strain of his stress alone.

"I'm so sorry." I began crying. "I tried! I tried, Austin, but he won't let me out and I don't know what to do. I was so ashamed to tell you. I never tell anyone."

He came back to me and dropped to his knees, gripping my face in his hands; one of them now covered in blood with fingers more than likely broken.

"My beautiful Brianna, don't cry," He began to soothe me, pressing desperate and unrestrained kisses against my lips, filling my mouth with the salty, metallic taste of blood and tears. "Don't be afraid, sweet girl. I'll take care of everything for you as I always have..."

His words only filled me with more fear as I noted the rapid change of his tone...and the slight British accent that had slipped out in his anger.

He walked over to his desk, wiping his face with the palm of his good hand. He pressed the button on his desk, "Regina, call Mr. Thomas and tell him to come to the studio *immediately*."

Trax

I slouched in the chair with my cheek propped against my fist, staring at Brie as Austin paced the room like a caged animal. Something was off about her, and I figured by the stiff, terrified way she sat and the fact that she wouldn't look at me meant I was about to be fucked over.

I glanced toward Austin then back at Brie.

"Someone gonna tell me what the hell is going on?"

Austin yanked his suit jacket off and tossed it over the back of the couch, then tore at his neck tie to loosen it clumsily, like he was using his unnatural hand.

"There's been a change of plans." He said, pacing back to his desk, attempting to steeple his fingers but quickly lowering his hands to the desk instead. I could see now that the fucker's swollen fingers were a fresh shade of dark purple and I lifted an eyebrow. "The final episode is going to be filmed as planned, but the marriage will not be registered with the State. After it airs, we'll tell the press that..."

"Whoa, whoa, hold up," I leaned forward. "You mean it's gonna be a fake wedding?"

Austin squinted at me, "No, it's going to be a fake *marriage*."

I turned my head to look at the gorgeous girl in the chair beside me.

She would have become my wife the next day, and I had been looking forward to it in a way I still can't wrap my head around. Knowing that wasn't going to happen now felt like a hard kick to the nuts.

"You're breaking contract," I growled out at the two of them.

What else was I supposed to say? The truth? That it was *breaking my fucking heart?* Screw that.

"We'll be negotiating a revised contract with your lawyers and you will be compensated for the inconvenience."

"Fuck the inconvenience. Fuck the contract. And *fuck you!*" I jump from my chair and turned to Brie. "Why are you so damn opposed to marrying me?"

She turned away, covering her mouth with her hand as she quietly sobbed, so Austin spoke for her. "She's already married."

I could tell by the tone of his voice it wasn't to him.

I shook my head. "I fucking *knew* you'd pull this shit."

I walked out of the office, slamming the door behind me.

I walked out of the building and hailed a cab, mumbling the address to the hotel I had been staying at. The hollow ache in my chest nagged at me to start drinking until I blacked out.

I stared out the window.

I had been so close. *So fucking close.* To what? What the fuck had I been close to?

Marrying Brie? Marrying *anyone*?

She was never in this to marry me. Hell, she didn't even *pretend* to want to marry me.

It was the actual, literal, goddamned reason I fell so hard for her—because she didn't try to impress me and that made me look harder at what I was missing out on. But, dumbass that I am, I didn't want to accept that she didn't give two shits about trying to impress me *because she didn't fucking want me*.

She had asked me again and again not to pick her, but I did. She lost control of the game and now she's trying to take it back with some bullshit story about already being married.

I'm sorry, but fuck that shit.

No normal guy would be okay with letting his wife date *me* on national television.

And she fucking kissed Austin!

She's not married—she's scared.

And I knew exactly how I was going to prove it.

"Driver; change of plans."

I stared across the counter at the dazed woman and smiled.

"Remember me?"

She emitted a squeal from the back of her throat, but didn't answer.

"I'll take that as a yes. You think maybe you and me could talk?"

The girl didn't move, just stood there wide-eyed and frozen. I looked around the room and ran my hand over my beard and mumbled, "What the fuck am I doing? This is bullshit."

A guy with no less than fifty piercings and blue spiked hair stepped up to the counter and pushed the girl aside, "Hi, may I help you?"

"Yeah, I was trying to talk to this one," I gestured toward the chick.

The guy bumped her shoulder with his then looked back at me. "Looks like Gabby's broken. Is there something I might be able to help you with?"

I looked around, lowering my voice, "Look, I don't care who the hell I talk to, I just want some answers about Brie."

"Brie?" Gabby shook her head, breaking out of her trance. *"Brie Rose?"*

"Yeah," I replied, tipping my head at her like she was a complete idiot. "Brie Rose."

"What kind of answers?" Blue-hair asked, leaning his elbows on the counter, raising a challenging pierced eyebrow at me. I got the distinct impression this guy was hot for my woman.

"Like is she married?"

Gabby and blue-hair looked at each other like they were searching for an answer neither one of them were sure of.

Gabby turned back to me, "I thought she was supposed to be marrying you."

"Yeah, so did I," I scowled, hooking my sunglasses in the top of my shirt. "What's her relationship with Austin?"

"Her boss?" Gabby shrugged. "I'm pretty sure he likes her, but as far as I know she isn't hooking up with him."

"Mmm," I responded with a grunt, folding my arms over my chest. Gabby's eyes fell to my biceps and she let out a sigh. I quirked a grin at her, "See something you like, sweetheart?"

She snapped her eyes back up to mine, "I, uh…you're just so, sooo…*you*."

I chuckled.

"Look, do me a favor and don't tell Brie I was in here asking about her, alright?"

Blue-hair asked, "Why do you want to know if she's married?"

"Because if she isn't, shit's gonna get real."

He began chewing at the metal bar in his lip and the sudden shift of his eyes made me suspicious.

"You know something," I squinted at him. "Spill it."

"So, okay, yeah. She's 'technically' married" he told us, using his fingers to make air quotes.

My spine stiffened and so did my expression. "Meaning?"

"Some guy she met in college a few years ago fucked her over after she had just started working here. From what I gather, he gave her this big sob story and talked her into getting married in order to get some kind of family inheritance or something, promising her that they would get an annulment right away afterwards. Then he turned around and refused to sign the papers and he's been refusing ever since. She saves up her tips for months then spends it all on sending the divorce papers over to him, even though she knows he'll just refuse to sign them."

"Mm hmm," I mumbled, noticing that Gabby was completely dumbfounded.

It obviously wasn't something Brie was very proud of if she went around hiding it from people—including me. But at least I wasn't the only one she had kept her little secret from.

I wanted to kill the fucker for wasting so much of her goddamned money, knowing how much she needed it. Not to mention that he was fucking with my life now, too.

"So like is she still in love with the guy or something?"

"Oh, hell no," Chase laughed, like it was a ridiculous assumption. "They never had a romantic relationship. She barely knew him. He literally played on her kindness and she though she was helping him. I have no idea why he ended up screwing her over after the fact, but he did."

"Motherfucker," I grumbled under my breath. "You know who this guy is?"

Chase shook his head, "She's never told me, but if I ever find out, I'm first in line to kick his ass."

I slowly squinted at him and he rolled his eyes, "She's my best friend, and yeah, I'd fuck her, but I don't intend to unless *you* fuck things up with her, *Rock Star*."

I laughed. I should hate this guy, but I couldn't.

"So wait," Gabby finally found her voice. "I'm confused. If

she's already married, that means she can't marry you on the show."

"Yeah, no shit," I sneered.

A grin crept onto her face, "And that pisses you off!"

"And that makes you smile?"

She clapped her hands together, bouncing on her toes. "Because you love her!"

I rolled my eyes, grabbing my sunglasses from my shirt. I put them on my face, "I'm out of here."

Chase narrows his eyes at me, "If you fuck with her, I'll beat your ass."

I leaned forward, "Ditto."

I peeled a fifty dollar bill from the roll of bills in my pocket and tossed it on the counter, grabbing a muffin from under a glass cake dome.

"Thanks for the info, blue-hair," I say, then winked at Gabby. "Keep the change."

I slammed open the exit door and hailed the next cab that came by.

Austin

"Neil."

The sound of my voice coming from the dark corner of his office made him jump and he quickly smacked at the lightswitch.

"Austin," he said, the quiver in his voice barely noticeable, but there.

He wasn't surprised to see me.

No, he was *expecting* my visit.

He moved toward his desk and bent down to push the security button underneath but my voice halted the movement of his hand, "I wouldn't do that."

He stood, casually adjusting his tie.

"So what brings you here?" He asked with a tight smile, just like we were old fucking friends.

"Have you seen the show?" I rose from the chair and slowly moved toward him.

His hands were visibly trembling.

He shook his head, laughing nervously.

"Nah, I haven't had a chance. Been helping Ma around the house while she's been sick."

His lips twitched in nervous response to my hard gaze.

"So how's it been going?" He asked, his eyes searching the desk for a way to defend himself. "I heard it's been blowing up in the ratings."

I quirked half a smile at him. "It's been just fan-*fucking*-tastic watching the woman I love slowly falling in love with another man, thanks for asking."

"Got yourself a woman, then?" He laughed, but I was not in a joking kind of mood.

"Yeah," I chuckled darkly. "But as it turns out," my eyes pierce him, "she's already married."

"Huh, how about that," he said with a nervous laugh. "To who?"

"A dead man."

I savored the moment his expression changed and he knew he was fucked.

His hand flex under the desk, pushing the security button like it was the life-line it was supposed to be. I reached into the back pocket of my jeans and pulled out a pair of wire cutters, snipping them in the air at him with an icy grin.

"I've had plenty of time to come to terms with your betrayal, Neil. Otherwise I might have put a fucking bullet in your head and quickly ended this shit. But what kind of friend would it make me if I didn't give you the chance to beg for my forgiveness?"

"Wh…what are you talking about?" He stammered, his eyes flicking over to the chair I had been sitting in. "What the fuck is that rope for, Austin?"

Ignoring him, I jumped over the desk and sat backwards in his lap, my knees pinning his hands and arms into his oversized leather desk chair, gripping him by his collar as I pressed the wire cutters high into his left nostril until he grunted in discomfort.

"You took something that belongs to me, didn't you, Neil?" I whispered against his face, an angry tear sliding over my cheek and onto his.

"I had no idea, man," he stammered. "I had no idea, I swear it!"

"I told you to stay the fuck away from her," I growled, saliva dripping from the corner of my mouth onto his shoulder.

"I haven't gone anywhere near her, I swear! The marriage was a scam! I just wanted her money, that's all! I swear, I never even touched her!"

I shook my head in disappointment, "I don't believe you, Neil."

"I swear! I swear I never laid a finger on her! Ask her! Just ask her!" He cried as his body shook with fear. "I'll sign the papers right now! Just give them to me and I'll sign them!" He was sobbing…pleading, "I swear, man, I didn't mean anything by it." I shoved the cutters higher into his nostril and he cried out. "I'll sign the damn papers, just let me go, please, Austin…I swear, I swear…"

I was breathing heavy, using all of my strength to keep him from pushing me away. There was no way for him to defend himself. Nothing for him to grab, no way he could escape without losing his entire nose in one flick of my wrist.

"Did you fuck her?" I murmured in his ear softly, like a scorned lover.

I had him gripped so tight that he could only shake his head with small jerks.

"No, no, never. I swear. I never touched her," he cried. "Ever!"

"What kind of husband never fucks his own wife?" I asked calmly, opening the wire cutters and forcing them into his two nostrils. "Do you smell bullshit?"

I squeezed them closed, feeling the soft cartiledge split like thick leather beneath the blade. He screamed out in pain as blood began pouring out in buckets down the front of his shirt and mine. He sobbed and I opened them again, pushing them higher up his nose, "Did you take her innocence, Neil?"

"No!" I squeezed them shut again and he screamed out, sobbing through the gurgling of blood in his throat, "I tried, but she didn't let me."

"Motherfucker!" I yelled, jumping off of his lap and punching his face hard with the wire cutters still in my grip. I kicked him hard in the stomach, the blood loss causing him to fall forward out of his chair. I paced across the room and grabbed the rope as he made a pathetic attempt to scramble for the door.

I tackled him to the floor, and when he was nearly unconscious from the blood loss and repeated impact of my fists, I grabbed the computer monitor from his desk and brought it down on his skull until I saw dark blood running out of his ears.

I tied one end of the rope to the leg of his desk and used a chair to break the window of his office. Dragging his limp body over to the window, I tied the rope around his neck and propped him up against the wall. I kicked his unresponsive body a few times to vent some of my still-unresolved anger, but it wasn't enough.

Dead wasn't enough.

The motherfucker owed me—he fucking *owed* me.

I knelt beside his body and poked him with my finger as I hissed, "Fuck you, Neil, you dirty backstabbing piece of shit."

I saw his fingers twitch so I dragged his body up to the broken window and pushed.

I wiped my blood-covered hand over my face. A grin tugged at the side of my mouth as I peered down at his body convulsing in jerks, mid-way between the fourth and third floors.

I slammed his office door closed.

My sweet Brianna. See how I make all of your problems

disappear?

I'm your hero. Your savior.

And you—you're my *possession.*

In the elevator, I slowly licked the salty blood from my fingers; my eyes closed as I think about the plans I have for tomorrow.

My lovely, innocent Brianna.

Tomorrow, after the final show is filmed, I will be moving you to the safety of our castle where nobody will ever be able to try and take you from me again, and I will slowly savor peeling away the innocence that you have saved for me and we will live happily. ever. after.

Brianna

Wanda had painted my nails the same lime green color my boots had been on the first episode.

I just want to surround myself with that color all of the time because it reminds me of brand new leaves and fresh cut grass. It gives me hope and energy when life feels like a perpetual winter.

But today the color was failing me and winter was everywhere.

The worst of my fears had passed after telling Austin I would not be able to marry Kevin.

While I had believed that breaking my contract would financially ruin me, in the end it hadn't. Austin had taken full blame for coercing me into agreeing to do the show without regard to my very obvious protests, so he had the contracts amended.

For that, I was truly grateful.

Kevin, on the other hand… what could I even say to him?

I had truly enjoyed his company and I felt terrible that things between us had to be ending the way they were. After today's episode was over, there would have been little chance that we would have kept in contact anyway.

What we had shared was meant to be short-lived.

I didn't fit into his rock star lifestyle, and he didn't fit into my yet-to-be-determined plans.

What also tugged at my heart was knowing that this would also be my last day of being at the studio. My internship was finished and I had received my degree. It was time for me to pick up and move on from my life in Los Angeles.

It was extremely unlikely that I would see anyone from this studio again, and it was a bittersweet feeling knowing you were going to be saying goodbye to people for the last time.

Although this wedding episode should be marked in celebration of a successful first season, a looming sense of worry darkened my mood.

Filming would begin within the hour, but there was nothing about acting the part of a bride that appealed to me—especially knowing that the country believed the wedding to be real.

When the press leak made its way out sometime in the next week—that there was a problem filing the paperwork—the entire show was going to implode. I had no doubt what would be coming on the tail end of that and I just prayed that people showed mercy on me as I packed up and moved my life eastward.

My plan going forward was to file for a contested divorce and leave Hollywood behind so I could try to find purpose in what I was doing again.

But that didn't mean the viewers were going to forgive me, and I knew damn well that Kevin Thomas never would.

I heard the lock on the door of my dressing room click and turned to find Austin gazing at me with an easy, tilted grin. There was something about the steadiness of his eyes and the slouch of his body that made me suspect that he had taken some kind of medication to calm his nerves.

He took several slow steps toward me, his eyes falling to the terrycloth robe I still had wrapped around me.

"You look lovely, Brianna," he purred, his easy smile making my heart flutter.

My sixth sense swatted the fluttering sensation like a horse whip, killing it instantly.

"Thank you," I smiled at him, "I'm just waiting for Fabiano to bring me my dress."

He took a few steps closer, now entrenched in my personal space, making heat rise into my cheeks. He lifted his knuckles and rubbed them slowly against my cheek as he held my eyes with his. What had felt like fluttering only moments before now felt like the scrambled beating of wings trying to escape in fear.

His eyes.

They were unmistakably dead. Motionless. Intent. Possessive. Crazed....

This was not the effects of any medication...*this was obsession.*

He pulled the ties of my robe and it fell open. For the first time while being alone with him, I felt as if I might be in danger. Whoever *this* Austin was; he was not the one I had known.

He slid his hands around my bare waist and pulled me closer, pressing his lips to my neck.

"What are you doing?"

"Loving you." He trailed kisses down my neck; hands groping at me possessively as I attempted to ease him away from me.

"What?" I gasped; a quiet, possessive growl rumbled from his chest, sending a chill through my body as he slowly slid a single finger between my breasts.

"Neil took something that didn't belong to him." He said

against my ear, causing me to freeze. I had never told him Neil's name. "You're mine, Brianna. *Only* mine."

"What…what did you do?" I swallowed hard—terrified of the answer.

"I killed him." He whispered with an easy smile, pulling a thumb over my bottom lip and holding my eyes with his. "For you…"

"No," I shook my head, trying to un-hear what he had just said.

It wasn't possible.

Clearly a figure of speech.

There was no way he would have actually *killed* Neil.

Nobody actually *killed* anybody in *real* life.

It had to be an exaggeration, a phrase, an expression…not literal…not murderous…

And yet…his eyes.

His eyes.

Dead.

Like Neil, the voice of truth inside me whispered.

I wanted to run, scream, escape, but I didn't know what this man was capable of doing to me.

Would he kill me, too?

I thought back to when I had shot that video of Mika. She had told me in her experience it was better to play along with the mentally ill than to challenge their delusions.

"What about the final episode?" I asked, trying to steer the conversation away from Neil.

Something changed in him and he slowly pulled away from me, eyes shifting between mine with uncertainty, his hypnotized grin slowly fading.

I knotted the ties of my robe tightly, trying to hide my trembling.

I stood there, watching him taking backward steps. Some variation of normalcy resurfaced in his eyes as he looked around the dressing room in confusion.

He ran a hand over his face, uncovering an alluring smile.

"Shit, Brianna, I forget what I was supposed to tell you." He let a quick laugh escape, "Fabiano sent me in here to tell you something." He snapped, remembering, "He said he'd be here with your dress in about fifteen minutes."

He walked to the door.

"Don't be nervous," he said, looking back at me. "It's not a real wedding, today."

He pulled open the door, "I'll see you on set."

When he closed the door behind him, I sat down and let out the long, hysterical breath that had been held captive inside of me. I did everything I could to keep myself from crying, but my heart would not stop pounding against my chest.

Austin was so incredibly gone that he had changed personalities right in front of me.

I had no choice but to believe what he had said about Neil —that he even knew of him in the first place was questionable enough, and now the possibility that he was *dead?*

I felt myself hyperventilating.

I ran to the door and slowly opened it, peeking down the hallway in both directions.

When I saw the coast was clear, I darted toward Kevin's dressing room, placing my ear against the door to make sure he was alone before quietly knocking.

When he pulled it open, I shoved him inside, locking the door behind me.

Trax

"What the hell's going on?"

Brie pushed me into my dressing room and locked the door behind her like someone was chasing her. To say she was freaking out was an understatement.

"I...Aus..." she was breathing so rapidly I wasn't sure how she hadn't hyperventilated yet.

"Sit down," I said, coaxing her toward the couch. "You gotta try to get a hold of your breathing or you're gonna pass out."

She sat and leaned forward, trembling and hiccuping between dry heaves. She was either in the middle of a full blown panic attack or coming down off of a major high.

I slid my arm over her back, "Babe, I got you. Calm down."

She turned and curled into my body, clinging to me like she wanted to hide inside of me.

"Is this about the wedding?" I asked, trying to figure out what had her so upset.

She shook her head furiously.

"Aus...Aus..." she gasps.

"Austin?"

She nods.

"Did he say something to you?"

She went to dry heave again, and I let her. I could have cared less if she puked on me as long as she was letting me hold her. I rubbed her back for several minutes and eventually her breathing began to slow. A loud knock at the door had her tensing up again and she dug her fingernails into me, making me cringe at the pain.

"Yo!" I shout.

"Have you seen Brianna?"

Hearing Joelle's voice, Brie's grip on me loosened a little.

"Yeah, she'll be there in a few."

"Alright, try to make it quick. This dress has a thousand buttons!"

"Gotcha!" I reply.

I tipped Brie's chin up with my finger and whispered, "Baby, tell me what happened."

"He's insane," she hissed, wide eyed and nervous. "He came into my dressing room and..." her breathing began to quicken again and she took a long pause to keep herself under control. "...he was acting really strange and then he told me..." she lowered her voice, swallowing back a lump in her throat, "...he told me he killed Neil. He knew his name, Kevin! I never told him my husband's name!"

"Bullshit!" I said, pushing up from the couch. "What the fuck, Brie?"

"I swear to you—I'm not lying."

It was clear as hell she wasn't lying, but why the fuck would he make shit like that up to scare her? What the hell was wrong with him?

"You honestly think he killed some guy? Come on. You can't really believe that."

"You didn't see him! He came in acting all weird and then something clicked and suddenly he was acting completely normal again, like he had no idea why he was even there."

I searched her eyes and sure as shit she was terrified.

"Fuck," I bite out, pissed at Austin. I cover my mouth with my hand, planting my other hand on my hip, "Alright, so now what?" I say, trying to reason with her. "What do we do? Did you call your husband to see if he's okay?"

She shook her head, "I left my phone in my dressing room."

I pulled out my phone, "What's his name? If he's dead, it would be all over the news, right?"

"Neil Malone," she said quietly.

I did a quick internet search and I could literally feel the color drain from my face when I saw the first news article. I stuffed my phone into my back pocket and paced to the window, wondering how long I had until I lost my shit like she did.

She could tell by my reaction that she didn't have to ask—my expression said it all.

"Oh my God," she whimpered, throwing a hand over her mouth and sobbing.

"Alright, calm down. Calm down. *Just calm the fuck down!*" I repeated anxiously, knowing that I was the one who needed to calm the fuck down.

There was suddenly another loud, rapid knock on the door, "Brianna! We have to get you dressed!"

"She'll be right the fuck there!" I barked out angrily.

I dropped to my knees in front of her, taking her hands and lowering my voice, "Alright listen. Here's what we're going to do. He's not going to hurt you. Not with a set full of people. We're going to fake our way through this episode because if you leave now you're going to have a shitload of people coming after your ass with lawsuits. We're going to shoot the episode and right before the after party, we're going to get you the hell out of here and go straight to the police. It'll be a good hour before he'll even know we're gone. You think you can do that, baby? You think you can make it through another hour in the same room as him?"

She nodded.

"Alright," I pressed a kiss to her forehead. "Let's go get married."

"But I can't stop shaking," she said. "Everyone will see."

"Brides are always nervous. Just go with that."

I honestly couldn't remember a damn thing about the last episode except the look on Austin's face throughout the entire shoot. He was watching her in a way that made me feel like shooting his psychotic ass so he couldn't hurt my girl.

After Brie left my dressing room, I pulled up that news article to read what the fucker had done and it was some sick shit. The fact that he walked out of the building at all was unreal. The crappy video footage from the security cameras in the lobby of the building had caught only the back of the man covered from head to toe in blood, and not one damn person said anything or got a license plate number?

Fucking Hollywood.

I didn't give two shits what was happening during the filming other than the fact that *one*; I wasn't going to let Brie out of my sight, and *two*; there was no way in hell I was going to put myself in the same room with him alone.

I'm manly as shit, but that motherfucker was certifiably insane and I knew he had a tangible kind of hate for me. I reached up and touched my nose, feeling myself cringe.

During the fake ceremony I repeated some words, Brie repeated some words, and the entire time my eyes kept shifting off-set, wondering at what point the fucker was going to flip his shit and point a gun at me.

If I had to put any money on it, I'd guess it was when I was supposed to kiss the bride. So as much as I wanted to finally plant my lips on hers, I realized it wasn't the best way to keep myself alive. So kissing the bride ended up being a chaste kiss right on her cheek.

After the end-of-season exit interviews with the host, Brie split her bouquet in half and tossed the halves toward Brandi and Tiffinni, making them squeal and reminding me that I had made the right decision, though not necessarily a decision that would benefit my health at the moment.

I leaned close to Brie's ear and whispered, "Alright, when they send us back to change before the after party, run in and grab your shit as quick as you can so we can get the hell out of here."

"I can't take this dress with me! It's tens of thousands of dollars to replace!"

"Fuck the dress, Brie! We'll mail it back to the studio after the fact."

"Fine," She nodded.

Heath called everybody together to congratulate the entire team, then invited everyone to a reception in the conference room. As people trolled around the set, cleaning up and putting shit away, Fabiano decided to follow the two of us toward the dressing rooms, fucking up our plans to get the hell out.

I followed them both into Brie's dressing room and Fabiano turned to me, "I have to help her unbutton this dress."

I crossed my arms over my chest, not going anywhere, "Go on then."

He lifted an eyebrow at me.

"I'm her husband," I sneered. "I can be here if I want too."

"Mm hmm," Fabiano said with a chuckle and began unbuttoning hundreds of tiny buttons. When she was free enough to step out of the dress, she pushed it down and grabbed her t-shirt, throwing it over her head before pulling her jeans on.

"See you at the after party, honeymooners," Fabiano left the room with a wave of his fingers. "Don't be late."

Brie grabbed her purse and we both rushed down the hallway toward the exit. Just as we were about to push open the door, we heard Austin's voice, "Where the hell do you two think you're going?"

I slowly turned to him, hoping he wasn't pointing a gun at me. I breathed out a sigh when I turned and saw that he was just standing there with his hands stuffed in his pockets, but Brie was right; there was something seriously crazy about the look in his eyes.

Brie pointed over her shoulder toward the door, "I left my inhaler at home. Kevin was driving me back to my place to grab it."

Austin lifted a challenging eyebrow. "You don't use an inhaler.

"How the hell would you know?" I asked.

He smirked like I was an idiot, pacing slowly toward us. "Where are you going, Brianna?"

I pushed open the exit door, shoving Brie through and shutting myself in with Austin as she screamed my name and pounded on the door that was locked from the outside.

Austin charged at me and I turned to kick out my leg, my boot landing a blunt impact directly into his chest. He coughed furiously, dropping to the floor and allowing me the clean kick to his head that knocked him unconscious.

I turned and flew out of the exit, dragging Brie down the steps with me toward the parking garage. Jumping in my car, I threw my phone at her, "Call the police. Right the fuck now. Tell them everything you know."

I began driving—there was no way we were going to either of our homes until I knew it would be safe, so for the next half hour Brie was placed on hold several times before we were finally given confirmation that Austin had been taken into custody.

It was nearly 3 in the morning when I finally brought Brie back to my house in Brentwood.

I tossed my keys onto the table and turned to find her slouched against the wall.

I slid my arm beneath her legs and carried her up to my bedroom, lying her on the bed and covering her with a blanket. I kicked off my shoes and lay beside her, reaching over to stroke her hair before closing my eyes and letting exhaustion defeat me.

Brianna

20 years.

The words from the mouth of the judge echoed against the walls of my mind as he spoke them.

The case had been fast to come to trial because money speaks. Kevin's fancy lawyers pushed to have the case moved up because of his pending tour dates, and Austin's fancy lawyers pushed for a speedy trial so that there would be as minimal damage done to his reputation as possible.

Ridiculous, considering he had *murdered* a man in cold blood. But knowing Austin, his story would end up becoming a movie and he would make more money sitting in prison that I ever would working my ass off.

To be honest; I was horrified by what Austin had done to Neil—and even more horrified *why*.

It was definitely the *why* in all of this that bothered me the most.

A man violently lost his life for no other reason than that another man had become transfixed on me in an unhealthy way.

It was not my fault.

I had done nothing to encourage his insanity.

And yet I was the catalyst that had led to Neil's death, and that knowledge chipped away at my soul in a way nobody could understand and I had to find a way to make peace with it before I was ruined.

When Neil had refused to divorce me, he set off the chain of events that eventually led to his own death. He couldn't have known what would happen, though what I learned from Freddy's testimony was that he knew he had been playing with fire when it came to Austin, yet still he did not relent.

Even as Freddy unveiled every wrong that Neil had done to me, I couldn't find cause enough for Austin to do what he had done.

Yes, Neil had wronged me but he had also wronged Kevin.

It all came out in this trial—*everything*.

Neil had tricked me into marrying him for the money to pay his own tuition bills; for the money Kevin had given me for a studio.

And he had hidden all of it from me—*all of it*.

There had been no inheritance, as he had told me in Vegas. *I* was the inheritance he was going after. *My money.* Money I had never even known about.

Freddy was taken out of the courtroom in handcuffs, for his part.

I looked at Kevin but couldn't even imagine what he might be thinking.

Was he feeling angry? Betrayed by the people he had hired to look out for him? Did he feel as stupid and naive as I did for trusting the wrong people?

Austin stared at me the entire time I was testifying on the stand.

His gaze was so intense that I felt certain he had never blinked. The heat that filled me under his stare was terrifying because, even though the testimony I provided would lead to his conviction, his eyes were filled with admiration.

His gaze on me in that courtroom embedded itself upon my subconscious, and for weeks following the trial I woke in a cold sweat, seeing him hovering over me in my bed; in the dark.

I was terrified of being alone in all of those hotel rooms, and yet I knew if I were ever going to recover from my fears, I had to face them.

20 years for murder in cold blood.

How could this have been the same soft-spoken man I had worked for? Who had been stalking me at the coffee shop and had conveniently offered me the exact same job I was looking for…

It had all been a lie.

I had believed he was a good man.

I had almost gone out to have drinks with him! Hell, I even *kissed* him!

What might have happened if I had shared his bed?

Would it be *me* in that grave right now?

"Upon investigation," the man on the witness stand said, "it was discovered that the defendant's apartment was covered in hundreds of candid photos, personal effects, and documents dating back several years up until the present. All items were specific to the deceased's estranged wife; specifically a Miss Brianna Rose."

Kevin was leaning forward in his seat, his face hidden by his hand as he listened.

Why me? *Why me?*

It was the only question I couldn't seem to find an acceptable answer to.

There was nothing special about me. Nothing that should have driven this man to do what he had done or feel the way he felt. There was nothing extraordinary about me.

"Miss Rose, did you have any reason to suspect that the

defendant might be planning your husband's murder?"

"No," I responded, taken aback by the question.

The lawyer was trying to lead me. "Were you not *purposely instigating* the defendant by manipulating his jealousy? Did you not ask him 'take care of' the little 'divorce problem' for you?"

"It would have been nice if Neil would have willingly signed the divorce papers, but I would have filed for a contested divorce eventually."

"Eventually. As in; after Murray Studios sued you for breech of contract?" I glared at the lawyer. "Money is a great motivator, isn't it, Miss Rose?"

"I wouldn't know, I never had a lawyer's salary," I replied, glaring at the lawyer.

"So, tell me again," he said, retaliating. "How did you *not* know that your husband and your boss were well-acquainted? *Friends,* if you will."

"I didn't know anything at all about the man I was married to, let alone the people he knew. I told Austin that I was married because I had to. I had no idea that he knew my husband or that he would be crazy enough to go and kill him!"

"Objection!"

"Sustained."

My eyes fell on Austin's as he gave me the most beautiful and sincere smile an obsessed murderer could give another person.

After a dozen more accusatory questions that were intended to point a guilty finger at me but failed to convince the jury, the defense attorney said, "No further questions."

As I was escorted from the stand and back to my seat, Austin looked up at me with adoration in his eyes as he whispered the words, "I'll find you."

Only as I was walking out of the courtroom with his

sentence in place did it fully hit me what Austin had said.

He'll find me.

Find me when?

My heart began to race as I realized that 20 years wasn't *life* in prison. He would be released someday. A lot of people get out well before their time is even served.

This man—*this crazy, obsessed man*—would be out of prison by the time I was 44 years old; if not sooner...

He'd have nothing to do in prison except obsess upon his obsession.

Carve a deeper need—form a deeper hate.

It wasn't as if the system would make any effort trying to treat his mental illness. He would come out even more deranged than he was going in.

And he would find me.

I felt like I was going to faint when I felt Kevin come up beside me and wrap his arm under mine to hold me up. I placed a hand to my forehead, finding my balance, "I'm okay." I said quietly.

I continued walking toward the door and Kevin reached over to take my hand.

Austin became suddenly violent and had to be restrained by several guards.

"You're mine, Brianna!" He yelled out. The judge pounded his gavel and chaos ensued. When the guard opened the courtroom door for us, Austin became even more violent, "I will find you and I will fuck you into the grave!"

I continued walking forward without turning back to look at him.

The courtroom doors closed behind us and I collapsed in Kevin's arms.

The sound of Kevin's feet on the bare wood floors of my apartment should have alerted me to his nearness, but I was numb to everything.

His hand slipped onto my shoulder causing me to startle before he rested his chin on the top of my head. "You're really leaving?"

I nodded, never pausing long enough to let my emotions catch up with me.

It had been too much to process.

Neil. The trial. Austin's threat.

Even Kevin, in some regard.

He wanted to be there for me, but all I wanted to do was keep everyone as far away from me as possible. I wanted to get away. Leave. *Run.*

How often had Austin been lurking outside of this apartment?

How many times had he actually broken in?

There was no way of knowing.

And Neil.

If he had never coerced me into that stupid marriage, maybe he'd still be alive.

I hadn't known him very well before, and I certainly hadn't liked anything about him afterward. But nobody deserved that sort of end.

How long until I met *my* end? *...20 years...* the quiet voice inside of me answered.

Panic taking over, I began throwing more things into open boxes.

I had to get out of this apartment. The walls felt closer than they ever had before.

His eyes has been everywhere.

I felt my skin crawling.

He had followed me—*watched* me for years...*years!* And I had never known.

I felt bile rising in my throat and began tearing up again. My body trembled, fluctuating between waves of shivering cold and sweaty heat.

Sensing my distress, Kevin wrapped his arms around me, holding my arms tight to my body.

"Breathe, little girl," he whispered into my ear, holding me until my trembling subsided.

When he finally let me go, I sniffed and wiped the wet from my cheeks.

"I'm fine," I whispered, unable to find strength in my voice.

"You're *not* fine," he corrected me. "You need to get your ass to a fucking therapist."

"No," I refused, continuing to pack. "The last thing I want to do is talk about any of this."

He let out a loud sigh but didn't say anything else.

As Neil's legal widow, I learned that I had been entitled to all of his personal and financial assets. In the end, though, I only kept enough of his money to return what Kevin had fronted for the two of us, despite his protest in accepting it.

Everything else went to Neil's mother, who was irate when she found out that her beloved son had been secretly married to a *thief* who *stole an old woman's inheritance* and threatened to sue.

Turns out that bad apple hadn't fallen far from the family tree.

Kevin had talked me into holding onto Neil's studio—which was actually *my* studio—until I decided whether or not I would ever return to film-making, so I turned temporary control over to the current employees, caring very little whether they sank it or made it thrive.

A notification came through on my phone.

"My ride is here."

"Please, let me come with you." Kevin pleaded. "I need to know you're going to be alright."

I shook my head, grabbing up a duffel bag that contained

everything I needed.

"You're going out on tour in a few days. Wherever I end up, I'll be fine."

The movers were going to be collecting the rest of the boxes and taking them to a storage unit until I found a permanent place to live.

"Brie, look at me," he lifted my chin and stared into my eyes. "Whatever this is between us…I don't want to let it go."

I shook my head. "Kevin, we're just friends…"

"Then be my friend, Brie," he said.

I nodded, "Okay."

He pulled me into a hug and kissed the top of my head.

"Take care of yourself," he murmured, sliding the duffel bag from my shoulder, slinging it over his.

I locked the door behind us and he walked with me down to my waiting cab. He opened the cab door for me and I slid in, putting my bag on the seat beside me.

I looked up at him as he closed my door and leaned in through the window, holding his lips against my forehead for several moments.

Then he stepped back onto the sidewalk, lifting his hand in goodbye as the cab pulled away.

Trax

It had been 118 days since I let the woman who had turned my life on its axis drive away in that cab, and 117 since I've been sober.

I had now been apart from Brie longer than I had actually been a part of her life, but the wound she left in me was still bleeding out in the form of dark amber liquid.

I didn't know where she was, or if she was okay.

One minute she was part of my life, the next she was just gone.

No forwarding address. No idea where she was headed. She just ran, and I didn't know if I'd ever see her again. The idea that I might not was crippling to me.

I had never done relationships. I had never done *love*.

I had no idea how to move on. Hell, I didn't *want* to move on. I just wanted to see her, hear her voice—even if it was just to tell me to fuck off.

I tried calling her every night the first couple months, but her phone always went straight to voicemail that I eventually filled up with half-drunk ramblings.

All of the text messages I sent are still hanging out in *unread text purgatory,* and every single thing about that leads me back to the same conclusion; she doesn't want to hear from me.

She had tried to make that fact crystal clear to me when she was leaving, but I wouldn't listen—I didn't want to believe that what we shared was something she could easily walk away from.

But she did.

Every time I wonder if I'm the only one she's been ghosting and dial the coffee shop where she used to work, I realize I'm too afraid to know the answer to that question so I hang up. I fear the answer to that more than I fear the silence. As long as there's a chance she's still out there finding her way back to herself, then there's still hope that she'll find her way back to me, too.

She has to.

She fucking has to.

Now that the band was back out on the road, I felt her absence beneath my hands every night that I played up on that stage. It's been nothing but empty movements of my fingers over the strings. Playing all the songs perfectly by heart, just not *with* it anymore.

I was cheating everyone.

While half our fans were too wasted and the other half were too amped up on the rush of the show to notice the difference; it was my band who had called me out on my shitty attitude and drinking problem. They said I was half-assing the music because I was whole-assing the whiskey.

And they were right.

I had been trying to keep her absence to a whisper only to wake up every morning with a jackhammer pounding at my skull.

Only this morning I was also dealing with the goddamned misery of a tattoo that had been burned into my shoulder while I had been stoned out of my fucking mind last night.

"What the fuck," I hissed, twisting to look down at my shoulder. I pulled off the bandage that had been covering an ornate thorny rose with the name *Brianna* carefully inscribed within the stem.

I ran my fingers delicately over her name, wondering just what kind of shady tattoo artist made house calls to wasted celebrities who are clearly too intoxicated to think straight. At least whoever the fuck it was had done an amazing job.

"Where the fuck are you, Brie?" I growled, letting my head fall back onto the pillow and covering my eyes with my forearm, stretching the freshly inked skin of my shoulder and making it burn again. The burn was nothing compared to the dull ache in my chest.

I was too tired to get out of this bed.

Adding to my growing list of *too tired*'s.

Tired of being on the road.

Tired of living in motels and on buses.

Tired of eating greasy fast food.

Tired of fame.

Tired of the expectations people had for me.

So fucking tired of playing music I no longer felt connected to.

Playing the guitar had always been my own personal form of communication with the rest of the world. Music was in me and it needed to come out.

But now there was a woman-shaped hole in my life and music didn't do shit to fill it.

It was the awakening I had always feared, and realization hit me like a ton of bricks the moment she walked away; I was in love. I was in-*fucking*-love with the woman.

And she was gone.

The first time she made me laugh, my music had changed.

But now, without her, there was no music at all.

Brianna

I couldn't get him out of my mind.

Believe me, I had tried.

I had spent the first two weeks after leaving L.A. driving East, hoping that some town along the way would feel like home to me. But the more I drove, the more I realized that no place could feel like home as long as my demons were travelling with me.

Fear, shame…*guilt.*

Even in the middle of the country, I was recognized more often than I was comfortable with.

I dyed my hair auburn and soon took to wearing sunglasses; rain or shine. And to those who saw past my disguise, I simply lied.

It was exhausting, hiding from who I was and running from feelings I had tried to deny.

I hadn't understood the feelings that Kevin and I had developed for one another so quickly and had a hard time believing he had been as invested as he had proclaimed. Now that I was a part of his past, I had no reason to believe he wouldn't forget all about me as he slipped back into the rocker lifestyle.

It's why I hadn't spoken with him.

It's why I hadn't read or responded to any of his messages.

I wanted to prove to us both there had been nothing there; that we had been bonded by a trauma we'd both prefer to forget.

But the longer I wandered aimlessly in search of myself, the more I was discovering that I would never find who that was without facing my feelings for him.

I pulled my car to the side of the road and pulled out my phone. The signal was just strong enough to allow me to do an internet search for Kevin's tour dates.

As if fate had led me to the place I needed to be that night, I found that Chevron Dreams would be playing to a sold-out arena three hours North of the town I had just passed through.

I put my phone away and began driving toward the city, praying that someone in the parking lot would be selling tickets.

As nervous and excited as I felt at the prospect of seeing him, he had gone silent in the last month. Whatever pull he had felt between us, he had finally gotten past and there was no longer a chance for us.

I just wanted to see him without his knowing, from somewhere in the crowd. And when I could no longer bear the pain of seeing him; I would leave.

I couldn't blame him for giving up—I had forced him to.

I had given him no reason to wait for me.

When we parted that day I had intended to never to see him again, despite the fact that I had promised him my friendship. But a friend wouldn't ghost him when she's lost and trying to find herself. A friend would have taken his hand and let him guide her while it was too dark to see, instead of running straight into the dark, all alone.

No, I wouldn't let him know I was at the show.

I wanted to experience the man and the music that the entire world already experienced.

I wanted to hide in a sea of faces and let his presence fill the hole that had torn open in me these past few weeks.

…or feel it tear open even wider.

It was not something I had ever anticipated doing, nor would I *ever* be proud of it, but I was desperate and that somehow seemed to justify the decision in the moment.

I shoved several hundreds of dollars into a scalpers hand, nervously taking the concert ticket that would put me fifteen rows from the stage, hoping I didn't either end up in jail or find myself out of a fat stack of cash with a counterfeit ticket.

When I found my seat, it didn't take long for my body to react with shivers to the growing anticipation from all the people that were gathering in the stadium.

The people immediately surrounding me were amped up. Some of them were already drunk or drinking; some of them were giving me half-stoned smiles filled with confused recognition— offering me drinks and hits, all of which I politely declined.

They welcomed me into their party but never once asked me to confirm what it was they all suspected…if I was *her*.

Chevron Dreams hadn't even taken the stage and I was already shaking through the opening band's performance. I was stunned by the light show and all of the professional sound equipment. It had never actually hit me that Kevin's band was the real deal. They were the headliners; not a garage band playing at a local bar. This sold out arena was here to see them…to see *him*.

Just like me.

The only difference is, I was the only idiot in the place who hadn't been able to see him for the god he was.

No, I was the idiot who let him go.

The music drew out on one long final note and after a mumbled 'thank you' the stage lights darkened again and a wave of cheers sent the opening band toward the sides of the stage.

Several roadies set to work in the dark, replacing bottles of water, exchanging instruments, and adjusting the height of the microphone stand. All appearing like shadows, preparing the stage for what was about to come.

My heart began pounding so hard I wondered if I would be able to contain the sound of its thrumming even with tens of thousands of voices murmuring around me.

A long, loud whistle sounded out from the stands, creating a brief lull in the ambient noise of the audience as a dark shadow crossed the stage and took a seat behind the drum kit. The next shadow crossing the stage caused a slow growing whirr among the crowd, their volume increasing ten-fold as a third shadow picked up a guitar.

Then suddenly, all hell broke loose when the fourth and final shadow strutted confidently across the stage, taking his place at the center and throwing a guitar strap over his shoulder. He moved up to the microphone stand and hot tears began to stream down my cheeks before the lights even came up on his beautiful face.

My trembling hands covered my mouth as I began to sob like a crazed fangirl.

But I was more than just an emotional fan; I was a woman realizing that she was in love with a man she had let go.

The sound of an electric guitar suddenly ripped through the arena, followed by a roar of cheers.

The spotlight finally shone down upon him and strobes began flashing to the beat, accentuating his scruffy, masculine face.

The sound of his deep, gravelly voice vibrated through my chest and made my knees feel weak.

How would I ever be able to survive the next two hours?

How would I be able to leave and keep my heart from staying behind with him?

Song after song I suffered in the presence of his on-stage persona and I knew now—*I understood wholeheartedly*—why women swooned over him. I felt like even more of a fool for the dismissive way I had treated him on that show and every other time we had been together. I wanted to call Gabby and tell her; *'I get it, and you were so right!'*

My heart felt more and more hollow as I recalled the sadness in his eyes when he had begged to come with me wherever I went. I had put that sadness there; *I had wounded this beautiful god.*

The memory of the way his arms felt around me now collided with the strained tightness of his muscular face as he poured out his heart and soul for the world through that microphone.

Sweat glistened on his perfect body, the veins in his forearms bulging as he moved his hands over his guitar like music was his primary language.

I was barely an hour into the performance when my heart could no longer stand the pain of watching the man I had so foolishly given away.

I needed to find my way out of the crowd.

I needed to get some air.

I needed to get as far from this place as my car would drive me.

I needed to stop staring my biggest regret in his beautiful face.

I began politely pushing my way past the people in my row to get to the aisle when someone in the row behind mine yelled out, "Hey! You're that chick from the show!"

The two people at the end of my row turned, blocking my path forward to gawk.

"Hey, yeah—it is her! Does Trax know you're here?"

The music on the stage had paused between songs just long enough for several people in our row to call out in unison, *"Trax!"* Chaos began to ensue and despite my protests, they wouldn't stop calling out and pushing me closer to the stage. As more and more people in the crowd joined in calling out his name, I saw Kevin put his hand to his forehead to shade his eyes from the glaring spotlights.

The moment he recognized me in the center of the chaos, he spoke into the microphone, "Holy shit, guys! Give her some space. Let her through, will you?"

Kevin nodded to security and quickly took his guitar off, setting it on the guitar stand before jogging back to the edge of the stage. He waved me in as a security guard helped me under one of the crowd control ropes, sending me over to the edge of the stage.

Kevin held his hand out to me and pulled me up onto the stage.

He was panting slightly from performing, smiling at me through his exhaustion. "I am so fucking happy to see you."

He pulled me into a damp hug and I let my tears fall as he rocked us from side to side. The crowd roared and cell phones lit up the arena.

As I pulled away, I noticed the guitar player grinning at me from behind Kevin, like he knew exactly who I was.

"You okay?" Kevin yelled beside my ear so I would hear him through the noise.

I wiped my wet face and nodded, smiling. He took my hand and pulled me toward the center of the stage and grabbed the mic from the stand as he pulled me into his side, "Who remembers my girl, Brie?"

The crowd went crazy with cheers as I felt my face turn a bright shade of red under the teal stage lights and his adoring smile.

After the final episode, a press release was supposed to

have gone out clarifying that there had been some paperwork complications that voided the marriage, but with Austin's arrest and hasty trial, the press release never happened. Rumors spread like wild fire after the fact and the actual status of our relationship was still speculated about in the tabloids.

My appearance on stage would most certainly create a new buzz in the headlines for Kevin's band and it most certainly blew my disguise.

Kevin leaned in toward my ear, "We've got two sets until intermission. Will you wait for me backstage?"

I nodded and he smiled, pressing a long kiss against my forehead causing another wave of cheers among the crowd.

"Jake will take you backstage." He nodded toward a roadie waiting off-stage.

I glanced back over my shoulder at Kevin, noticing him watching me walking away with an appreciative head tilt.

"Damn, you've got a nice ass," he says into the microphone, shaking his head and causing the crowd to roar with applause as I smile back at him. "I hope I can remember how to play."

He plays the first riff of their most popular song *Bring it Back* and the crowd loses their mind.

The band played several more songs as I watched from the side of the stage. I didn't fail to notice how much more animated Kevin had become since I had been outed by the crowd.

The roadie, Jake, came up beside me and folded his arms over his chest as he watched the band. He grinned over at me, shaking his head, "Listen to him shred. You lit him on fire tonight. He's been a bit of a wanker past few months. I guess we know why."

I stared at Kevin as he played, fascinated by every little thing that I had never noticed about him before. And for the first time since I had left L.A., I wished I could capture this moment on video.

Kevin jogged off the stage and pulled off his rust-colored plaid button-down shirt, tossing it aside. He lifted the bottom of the t-shirt he was still wearing and wiped the sweat from his face, exposing his well-defined abs.

One of the roadies handed him a bottle of water and he chugged it down in one go as someone else from the stage crew asked him a question that held his attention.

He grinned and spoke expressively with his hands, looking every bit the rock star that I had never comprehended him to be.

His eyes swept the area and stopped when they landed on me; his grin widening.

Band members trolled around backstage stretching, using the bathroom, texting and chatting with members of the opening band and the stage crew. I was a stranger; completely out of my element, yet blending into the background.

Staying out of the way came second nature to me after working at the studio.

The studio.

I dropped my eyes to the floor to stave off the panic attack that I felt creeping up on me. They had been coming often, despite knowing that Austin was safely behind bars. A pounding ache formed in my chest and I felt short of breath as the words that would forever haunt me echoed in my ears.

I. Will. Find. You.

I felt him everywhere. Watching me. Always watching me.

Kevin slipped his arm around my waist, startling me from my thoughts.

"How the hell have you been, Brie?"

"Great," the smile didn't reach my eyes as I quickly wiped

a tear from my cheek.

He circled to stand in front of me and drew his eyebrows together, "What's going on? Talk to me."

"It's nothing," I laughed, waving off my emotions as I sniffled.

He bent his knees, meeting me at eye level, "Baby, you're crying."

I shook my head, slipping my hands around his waist and resting my head on his sweat-dampened shoulder, "I'm just really glad to see you."

"Two minutes!" A voice shouts somewhere backstage.

He pulled back, taking my face in his hands, "I don't want you to leave. Stay here, okay?"

I nodded, forcing a smile, "I will."

His eyes lingered upon mine...*searching*.

"Don't leave." He reiterated, "I mean it."

"Yo, Trax! Let's move!" A voice yelled.

He backed away, watching me warily as he headed toward the side of the stage. In a matter of seconds the volume of the crowd lifted, the first notes of his guitar rang out and I could no longer hear the rapid pounding of my own heart.

Trax

I gave the fans everything I had tonight.

I had a shit ton of energy and hope, and the whole arena felt it.

Drenched in sweat, my throat nearly raw from singing, I grabbed the water by Zach's drum kit and emptied it in one tilt. My arms and wrists ached in the best damn way they had in a long time.

I love this shit; *live for this shit.*

But tonight there was someplace more important I needed to be, and if I didn't call it after three encores, these greedy motherfuckers would have had us playing for them until the end of time.

When the show was done, I couldn't get off the stage fast enough, but she wasn't anywhere to be found. Jake was shouting orders to people behind a wall of amps and I yelled out over the noise of our cheering fans.

"Where's she at?"

"I don't know, man." He held his arms wide, like she had disappeared into thin air. "She was here for a while. Don't know where she went."

"Did she look pissed?"

He shook his head, "Naw, man, sorry. If I see her, I'll let her know you're looking for her."

I began walking away, my boots stomping across the concrete floor harder than usual.

"Fuck!" I spit out, my eyes searching for her everywhere as I pushed through stage crew who had already started tear down. "Please, baby, don't do this to me." I growled under my breath, shoving a hand through my sweat-soaked hair.

"Hey, Zach," I gripped my drummer's arm, getting his attention. "You seen Brie?"

"You mean the little girl you pulled out of the audience?" He grinned at me.

"Have you seen her?" I repeated with a growl, not in the mood for his shit.

"Sorry—try asking her babysitter," He smirked, pissing me off even more.

My pulse was racing faster and faster at the possibility that Brie had left even after she fucking told me she'd wait for me.

I pushed through the crowded hallway toward the dressing room, where several pretty girls waited outside the door, hoping to be invited in. I tipped my chin at them politely then pushed open the door. Digging through my backpack for my phone, my chest began to ache like a motherfucker when I saw there weren't any messages from her.

"She left me," I said out loud, wanting to punch the fucking wall.

My band mates began funneling into the room.

"Goddamn, Trax!" Paul bellowed, tossing his leather jacket across the back of a chair. "You tore through that guitar solo on *Leveled Up* like you were caught fucking it's teenage daughter!"

I kept my eyes focused on the floor. I had no idea what kind of noise would come out if I opened my mouth to respond.

"What's up with you, man?" He asked.

Zach answered for me, throwing himself back onto the couch and grabbing his notebook.

"Little Bo Peep lost his sheep, now he's going to spend the next four months as drunk as the last four."

"Fuck you," I growled, not even a little bit amused.

"So what was all that bullshit at intermission?" Paul asked. "Who was that chick?"

"Kevin's soul mate," Zach laughed as he scribbled in his notebook.

I was two seconds from punching Zach in his fucking mouth when Randy pushed open the door, pulling a girl by the hand behind him.

"I found this little stray hanging around backstage." Randy said. "Thought I'd take her home with me, if nobody else claims her."

"Shit, Brie," I said, releasing the tension in my sore muscles. "I thought you left."

"Yeah, he was being a whiny bitch about it, too," Zach said, twirling a drumstick in his fingers while flipping through his notebook, reading his scribbled notes.

I smacked the back of his head.

"What's so special about this chick?" Paul eyed her. "She looks like any other warm, wet hole to me, assuming she's even legal."

At the same time Randy audibly growled at him and bared his teeth, I jabbed my finger in his direction with a hard glare, "Watch your fucking mouth."

Paul held up his hands and widened his eyes, "Sorry man! Fucks your problem?"

Randy slid his arm around Brie's shoulder, his massive frame towering more than a foot above her. "Don't pay any attention to him. Our bassist is in rehab, so Paul's filling in.

He's a fucking colostomy bag." Brie raised an eyebrow and Randy explained. "A temporary asshole that's full of shit."

Brie sucked both lips between her teeth, fighting a smile.

"That ginger fuck over there is Zach." Zach lifted a drumstick in acknowledgement without lifting his eyes from his notebook. "You already know Romeo here, and I'm Randy—your biggest fan." He lifted her hand and kissed it, causing her to turn a shade of pink. "Miss Rose, you were fucking *lethal* on TV and I gotta be honest…I'm crushing hard on you. Especially with the red hair thing you got going on right now. If things don't work out with this piece of shit, I hope you'll consider giving me a chance."

"Shut the hell up," I said, removing Brie's hand from Randy's and giving him a long, hard look. "Don't let him fool you into thinking he's just joking. We're gonna head back to the hotel."

"I bet you are," Zach snorted.

"Sure you don't want to hang around for pizza?" Randy winked at Brie and I rolled my eyes. He'd never make a move on her, knowing she was mine. But he'd make it damn clear that he was interested, all the same.

"I got it covered, thanks," I replied, pulling Brie toward the door.

"Be sure that you do!" Zach called out behind us. "No reason to infect the little girl with all the nasty shit you're carrying."

I picked up a half-empty water bottle and chucked it at the back of his head, slamming the door closed behind us and pulling her by the hand toward the exit doors.

"Well, they were…interesting," she laughed as we walked.

"They're assholes," I grunted, looking back at Brie, suddenly realizing she probably didn't get here in a limo or tour bus. "Do you have a car?"

"Yeah," she said, tucking her chin length hair behind her

ear and pulling her keys from her pocket when we stopped at the exit door. "But I'm guessing you don't want to walk through a parking lot full of fans."

"There are usually about thirty people who hang around to meet us after the show. If you want to get your car and bring it around to the loading dock while I sign some autographs, we'll head out after that alright?"

She went to push the door open but I stopped her. "Brie…"

She turned and looked back at me.

I took a few slow steps closer to her. "Why'd you come tonight?"

"Because I missed you," she said, holding my eyes for a moment before she pushed open the door, disappearing into the waiting crowd.

You have no idea, little girl.

The minute I pushed open the hotel room door, I felt like an asshole.

I had forgotten what a lazy, piece of shit drunk I had become over the past few months and my room reflected as much.

I cleared my gravelly throat, "Housekeeping isn't allowed to come into our rooms."

"That's…unfortunate," Brie smirked.

I bent down to grab a handful of dirty clothes and tossed them in a pile beside the wall then started grabbing papers and shit from the bed and threw them onto the desk, trying to clear a place for her to sit.

Slowly trailing into the room behind me, Brie picked up one of a half-dozen empty whiskey bottles that were crowding the desk.

"Why are you not in rehab with your bassist?" She asked.

"It's not as bad as it looks," I winced, even though it was *every* bit as bad as it looked.

Heading to the dresser, I fished around and found a clean pair of boxers.

"I'm gonna hop in the shower real quick then we can talk. Go ahead and watch TV or something." I pulled out my wallet and tossed it to her. "Here, order up anything you want."

"Even a puppy?" She tilted her head, flashing me her sweet smile.

"*Especially* a puppy," I grinned at her, taking slow steps backward toward the bathroom door, trying to memorize the picture of her sitting on the bed.

She was *here*. Now all I had to do was figure out how to keep her from running away.

I had just finished washing the layer of sweat and concert funk off of myself when I heard the bathroom door open then quietly click shut.

I closed my eyes and let the warm stream of water rinse the shampoo from my long hair.

"I don't sign autographs on dick pics," I said as a grin tugged at the corner of my mouth. "You want to see what I got? You have to show me what you got."

When I opened my eyes, I saw Brie's fingers curl around the shower curtain and I froze.

She slid a bare leg past the curtain into the tub, followed by the bare rest of her.

I swallowed hard, forcing myself to speak.

"Well, shit, Brie," My voice came out gravelly as my eyes slowly trailed down her perfect body. "You're just full of surprises today, aren't you?"

She stepped closer to me, placing her hands onto my shoulders as she pushed up on her toes and cautiously pressed her lips against mine.

I slid my hand around the back of her neck, pulling her toward me and ravaging her mouth in desperation as the warm water streamed over us.

Finally. *Finally.*

The butterflies that she alone seemed to control went full flight inside of me.

I eased her against the wall, attacking her lips like I had been starving for them—and I had been for so fucking long.

"I missed you, Brie," I panted between long, sensual kisses. "So fucking much."

I slid my hands beneath her ass and lifted her against the shower wall when she suddenly broke away from my kiss.

"No, Kevin, wait," Her voice full of urgency.

I was panting—desperate and aching to be inside her. I lowered her feet back to the floor, kissing her again and making it hard for her to speak. I was pushing forward but she was still holding back.

"What's wrong, baby?"

She lifted wide, innocent eyes up to mine and whispered, "I don't want to lose my virginity in the shower."

Her vir…

My eyes held hers until I squeezed them shut, my mouth falling open as my body spontaneously reacted like a twelve-year-old boy to her words. When I opened my eyes again, I looked down at her belly and lifted the corner of my mouth in an embarrassed smile, "Sorry about that."

Brianna

I felt like such a child admitting the truth to him, but the truth was what it was. I hadn't necessarily been saving myself, I had just never had much of an opportunity to lose it. But now that the moment had come, I wanted it to be sensual and passionate; not heated and fast.

The entire night had been surreal.

Not even an hour earlier this same man was on stage in front of tens of thousands of screaming fans; admired and adored by all of them.

I hadn't ever known this side of him—not really. He had only ever been *Kevin* to me; never *Trax*.

He helped me over the edge of the tub and wrapped me in a towel, spinning me toward the door and urging me toward the bed with a slight press of his hand against my lower back.

With gentle fingers, he peeled that same towel from my body and let it drop to the floor, moving over me as I crawled backward onto the unmade bed. His eyes were glued to mine, burning with determination as I let my head drop back against the pillow.

His eager mouth claimed mine again; tired muscles causing his calloused fingers to tremble as they slid over my skin. His kisses soon slowed to gentle, sweet brushes of his lips against mine and I could feel his energy waning.

He traced his fingertips over my collarbone, eyes focused there as he quietly spoke.

"Brie, I need to tell you something."

I slid my hand over his cheek, drawing his gaze back to my eyes before he rolled onto his back, staring up at the ceiling. He began breathing more heavily, like he was fighting his emotions and losing.

"I can't do this anymore."

"Do what?" I rolled onto my stomach and propped my chin on my arm.

"Try to pretend that I'm okay without you, because I'm not. I'm fucking *not* okay, Brie. I'm in love with you."

I closed my eyes, fighting the tears that wanted to come.

"Stay with me." He said in a desperate voice, turning toward me so I could see the dancing flecks of blue in his hazel eyes. "Tell me you won't leave." He closed his eyes and tasted my lips with a slow kiss before he lowered his head to my pillow. "Promise me."

"I promise I'll stay," I replied, running my fingers around the angry red skin of the fresh tattoo on his shoulder. I tilted my head, squinting to read the small script writing that wrapped around the flower's stem: *Brianna.*

Trax

The last night of our tour is always one of our best shows, and we had been planning this one for weeks. After nine months of being on the road we were all feeling a little tour-worn. But tonight I felt a supernatural kind of high, not only from within myself but from the band and our fans.

Since joining me on tour, Brie had wrapped me around her little finger and there was no place else I would have rather been tied.

I never get tired of her kissable lips, of the way she makes me laugh, the way she can go from invisible to impossible in a matter of seconds.

She started shooting videos again and worked during the day editing clips from the tour into a video that we planned to release early the following year along with a twenty minute interview with me and the guys as a wrap-up to the *Bring it Back* tour.

Earlier that day I had met with the crew to go over the change we would be making to the tour's final show that night. We'd be switching out one of our regular songs for a new acoustic piece I had been working on and I wanted to make sure everyone was on board with the change.

The show went off without a hitch, and just before the last song in our regular set, we took a brief pause to let the audience's excitement build.

I set down my electric guitar and lifted my water bottle to my lips, glancing toward the side of the stage to make sure Jake had my back.

Brie stood there beside him looking like a fucking angel with that sweet little baby bump of hers—the one I had put there. My heart fucking soared.

I picked up my acoustic, throwing the strap over my shoulder trying to contain the shaking of my fingers as I mentally prepared myself for putting this new song out there for the whole world to hear.

I looked toward Zach and Steve, then at Randy who gave the nod to make it happen.

I stepped up to the microphone and spoke; my deep and gravelly voice quieting the fans to a low murmur.

"Tonight is the last night of our *Bring it Back* tour."

The fans go berserk like I expect them to whenever I say jack shit into the mic. My heart is thumping against my rib cage from the fucking adrenalin. "Y'all are gonna be the first ones to hear a new song we've been working on called *The Fifth Horizon.*" I strum a few notes as I speak. "It's about the kind of love that encompasses every corner of existence."

I glance over at Brie.

The crowd goes eerily quiet as a blue spotlight hits me and the stage lights fade out on the band.

I begin strumming my guitar at a pace that calms the racing of my heart as it breaks wide open.

As I begin singing, I wonder if I'll be able to get through the whole song without losing it, so I try not to listen to my own words—try not to feel their meaning.

Fuck. Tears begin blurring the edges of my vision. As long as they don't reach my voice, it's cool.

I know how many damn cameras are zoomed in on me—on the fact that I'm baring my soul for the first time ever in my music and I'm doing it live on stage.

When the hardest line hits me, my voice strains and cracks in a way that comes out spot-on for the emotions I've bled into this moment.

I couldn't look at her.

I knew I would fucking lose it, if I did.

After the last words come out, I turn my head toward her and smile through the pain, as the guitar melody beneath my fingers wraps up the last notes of the song.

Her hands cover her mouth and I know she's sobbing, but that's okay because—*fuck*—inside so am I, and so is the whole damned arena.

The music ends and the fans go profoundly quiet right before their sudden eruption.

I smile, glancing back at Randy who is giving me his characteristic nod of approval.

I step back out of the spotlight and turn toward the drum riser to wipe the wetness from under my eyes in way I'm hoping none of these eighteen thousand people picked up on.

I set down my guitar and walk across the stage toward Brie, holding out my hand for her to take then pull her into the center of the stage beside me; right into the spotlight the same way I had the first night she came back to me.

The crowd always goes fucking insane when they see her, and this time is no different. Every damn one of them knows the song was about us. Ours had been a love story that they had all been watching from the very beginning.

I grab the mic and take it off the stand, feeling Brie's hand nervously squeezing mine.

"What are you doing, Kevin?"

I ignore her.

"How many of you know my girlfriend, Brie?" I say into

the mic. The crowd roars in response. When I begin talking again there's a sudden hush, with only a few distant whistles making their way from the back of the arena. "A year ago, this girl did everything she could to get rid of me."

The audience laughs and she smiles tightly; her cheeks turning a bright shade of pink. She still isn't used to the spotlight so I pull her against my side, wrapping my arm around her waist.

"What's going on, Kevin? What are you doing?" She asks again.

I lift the mic to my mouth—again, ignoring her question.

"Six weeks after we met, I asked Brie to marry me," I look down at her with a smile and her eyes grow as wide as the fucking moon. "Back then she never gave me an answer, so I'm going to ask her again right here, right now. What do you say, Chicago? Should she take a chance on me?"

The fans go crazy as I get down on one knee before her, taking her hand. I deepen my voice and speak into the mic as I smile up at her. "Brie Rose, will you marry me?"

The crowd responds so loudly that part of me worries the roof wouldn't be able to withstand the noise. Brie leans in close to my ear, "I can't believe you're asking me on stage!"

I grin at her, "You're kinda leaving me hanging here, baby…yes or no?"

"Yes!" She laughs. "Of course! *Yes!*"

I drop the mic on the stage, stand up and grab her face, kissing her to the sound of cheers. When I finally let her go, I reach down and swoop up the mic.

"She said yes!" I bellow into the mic, creating the loudest roar of the night from the fans before grabbing her and planting another kiss on her lips. I kneel down and kiss her baby bump creating a new wave of cheers, letting my lips linger for a moment before standing to give her a hug.

"I love you, baby," I shout in her ear over the sound of the fans.

She presses her lips against my cheek, letting me know she heard me then suddenly pushs out of my hug, grinning from ear to ear as she grabs the mic out of my hand and speaks into it.

"Sorry, ladies."

The crowd cheers even louder for her than they ever have for us.

I give her another quick kiss and let her walk back to the side of the stage.

I whoop into the mic and punch my fist in the air several times, feet somehow still on the ground as they carry me back to my guitar stand. I pick up the guitar and throw the strap over my head and began fingering out the next melody as Zach picks up the beat to the last song on the schedule.

We rock that fucker into the ground.

Three encores and a few dozen autographs later, I'll have my girl all to myself for the rest of the night, the rest of the year…then for the rest of our lives.

Mostly.

Epilogue

Trax

I woke to the feeling of tiny hands pushing my long hair out of my face. The same tiny hands moved to my cheeks, squeezing my face between them until my lips pursed.

I opened one eye to find my beautiful little girl looking down and smiling at me beneath her own unruly brown curls.

I rolled onto my back and pulled her down against my chest in a tight hug, giving her a kiss on the top of her head and making her giggle.

"Where's Mommy?" I asked in a gravelly voice, stretching my free arm out and yawning.

"Out in the garden."

"In the garden?" I pretended to be insulted. "She didn't make us pancakes?"

"She said no pancakes until you wake up, so I'm waking you up. Up, Daddy! Up!"

The sound of someone playing drums in the studio drifted up the stairs.

"Is your brother playing around on Uncle Zach's drum kit

again?"

She smiled, shrugging.

I ran a hand through my hair, "We need to get that boy some lessons. Alright, I'll make you a deal. You tell Cole to lay off the drums for a while and I'll get up."

She skipped out of the room and I rolled to my side and sat up, scratching my neatly trimmed beard. I pulled on my jeans and walked over to the window, looking out toward the garden where Brie was pulling weeds in a lime green sun hat.

I smiled to myself.

God, I love that woman.

I love this life she gave me.

This family. *Our* family.

It's hard to believe there was ever a time when I thought music alone would make me as happy as I am now. I had been so fucking blind for so long. I live for playing and still crave the sound of screaming fans in a sold-out stadium, but that first laugh, first word, the first smile on each of our children's beautiful faces; just knowing that the woman I am so incredibly in love with said *I do* and actually meant it—that is fucking *everything*.

I made my way to the kitchen just as Brie finished washing her hands.

Our two youngest girls were snuggled close together on the couch and were watching their favorite video on the internet again. They've seen it a thousand times but can't get enough. I can't blame them—neither can I.

"Look! This is the part where Daddy tried to kiss Mommy right in front of the whole world!"

"She wanted me to kiss her," I said, grinning over at my beautiful wife.

Brie rolled her eyes. "I wanted nothing to do with you."

Coming up from behind, I grabbed her by the waist and wrapped my arms around her swollen stomach, feeling a little wriggle then a swift jolt against my hand; the new baby already siding with Brie.

"That's too damn bad, 'cause I wanted *everything* to do with you," I replied, trailing kisses up the side of her neck, making her skin warm.

She shushed me for cursing in front of the kids.

I fucking love this life.

From the Author

I hope you enjoyed my second published book, *The Fifth Horizon*. Keep an eye out for the sequel that brings the Thomas' oldest son, Cole (a lovable, foul-mouthed, raging *extrovert*) into his own romantic spotlight, while his parents' happily ever is falling apart. But they've had 20 years; *time's up*.

For something a little different, be sure to check out my first published book *August in New York* (a sweet, second-chance historical romance); also available on Amazon.

Join my mailing list at www.FioraMarkus.com.

I couldn't have gotten this far without my mentors, my muse, and my beta-readers, and I can't go any farther without my readers.

I appreciate you!
XO

Fiora Markus

www.ingramcontent.com/pod-product-compliance
Lightning Source LLC
LaVergne TN
LVHW050636100826
845148LV00011B/1879